The Best of

Frontier Tales

Volume 2

Winning short stories from
www.FrontierTales.com

Published by
Pen-L Publishing
PO Box 4455
Fayetteville, AR 72702

© Pen-L Publishing
All rights reserved
Design by Kimberly Pennell
Printed and bound in USA

First Edition April 2013

ISBN: 978-0-9851274-6-6

Cover art *Cowboys in the Bad Lands* by Thomas Eakins, 1888

Visit our web site at www.Pen-L.com

Dedicated to those who love the creak of saddle leather, a dance hall piano, and the smell of horse sweat and gun smoke. Saddle up for some fun times!

THE TALES

Firebaugh's Ferry

by John Putnam

It wasn't much of a town. The one ramshackle wooden building looked so poorly made that someone must've piled the barrels of beans, barley and wheat along the sides just to keep the place from blowing down in a good-sized wind. Next door a large round tent with 'saloon' scrawled in crude red letters over its open flap beckoned, and the rest of the posse ducked inside, their prisoner in tow. But I headed across the road to where wood smoke from a low chimney attached to a sod-roofed adobe carried the welcome smell of roasting meat.

I tied the mare to a rail, hopped down and pulled paper and pencil from my bags, then dodged a large trunk by the wall as I stepped inside. Indoors was refreshingly cool. Somehow this part of the world hadn't gotten the word that the seasons had changed and October shouldn't be as hot as July. There were four tables, two on each side of the door. A woman and boy were sitting to my left. I walked to the far right corner and pulled up a chair where I could see the flap of the saloon through the open window.

A small Mexican woman hurried up from the back wearing a grease-spattered gingham apron over a worn cotton dress, her hair tied in a red bandana, unease nestled in the corners of her dark eyes. "Buenos tardes, señor," she said in a trembling voice.

"Buenos tardes to you, señora," I replied, using almost all the Spanish I knew. I pointed to the fire in the back and rubbed my stomach.

"Hungry," I said.

"Oh, si, si," she gasped, seemingly relieved that I wanted food. "Carne asada con frijoles," she added.

I nodded eagerly. "Si," I answered. "Gracias. It smells good." I smiled honestly, happy at the prospect of a good meal for a change.

"Un momento, señor," she replied and hurried away.

I tossed my paper on the table and began to write. There was much to say. This was the end of the biggest story of my career with the Alta California and, in the twisted way we newshounds looked at things, was all because of my good luck. I'd been sent to the gold country to dig up colorful articles for the San Francisco readers, a kind of breaking in project for a new man fresh from the east. But no one expected me to fall right into the middle of the biggest manhunt this state had ever seen.

Tom Bell and his gang of hooligans had run roughshod over the territory around the Feather and Yuba Rivers for over a year, first robbing lone travelers along trails, then targeting the express companies that hauled in mail and supplies by mule to mining sites deep in ravines and canyons where no road existed and no wagon could go, then carried large amounts of gold back out. Posses had been sent from every town in the area—Downieville, Nevada City, Oroville—without finding a trace of Bell or his cohorts.

I'd had several dispatches that I wanted to get on the steamer to San Francisco as soon as possible so I had taken the Langston Company stagecoach south to Marysville. Later I learned it was at the California House stage stop in Camptonville when Tom Bell's spy had relayed information that the stage carried $100,000 in gold. Six of them hit us about half past four that afternoon, but the driver whipped the team right past Bell and two of his men who'd tried to block the road. The guard started shooting, the gang fired back, and several of the men in the coach joined in. We made as much speed as possible to escape the robbers, but two passengers and the guard were wounded, and a woman was shot in the head and killed outright. It was the first murder attributed to the Bell gang.

"Aquí, señor, carne asada, frijoles y tortillas." I near jumped out of my skin. I'd been wrapped so deep in my story that I hadn't noticed her coming with my meal.

"Gracias," I said as she put the plate in front of me, smiled awkwardly and backed away toward the rear of the café.

I dug into the food, rolling beef and beans together inside a warm corn tortilla, then ate it without a fork. My poor mother, bless her heart, would've had a conniption. I cleared the plate quickly, astonished at how hungry just riding a horse made me. But it had been a long ride, a month and a half, all the way from Marysville past Sacramento then many more miles south of Stockton to this God forsaken rat hole that scrounged its paltry existence from the few travelers who came here because a man name Firebaugh had started a ferry service across the San Joaquin River.

And it was the river that granted the only tinge of color to this whole drab world, with its clear blue water flanked by the green of sycamores and an occasional cottonwood. Everywhere else, as far as a man could see, there was nothing but dry, dead grass, brown dirt and dust. I shrugged; it was over now, I picked up my pencil again.

"Whatcha' doin', mister?" It was the boy from the other table. I smiled at him. "I'm writing a story for my newspaper," I explained.

"I can write," he bragged and grinned back at me.

"Tommy, leave the man be. Come back here and sit down." The woman, likely young Tommy's mother, spoke out from the far side of the room. The slow ease of her words suggested a southern breeding.

"He's fine Ma'am," I replied politely. "Seeing such a good looking, tow headed boy is a welcome change from the rough companions I've spent my time with lately."

"See Ma, I'm fine," Tommy whined.

"Do as I say, young man, right now," she barked, a no non-sense tone to her voice.

"Oh, Ma! I never get to do nuttin'," Tommy carped, but he shuffled back to her.

When I first walked in she'd been sitting with her back to me. Now she'd spun to shepherd her son and I stared deep into a sight little seen since this grueling chase had begun, a refined and gentle lady. A nose a tad too long coupled with a strong chin gave her round face an honest look in spite of the sadness of her expression. Auburn tresses curled loose below a dark green bonnet edged with lace, while a calico dress the color of a sweet honeydew melon barely concealed her shapely figure.

Yet nowhere about her could I see evidence of the hardship a life in this harsh country would impart on a woman. Her face and hands were smooth and free of the creases hard work and constant sun soon bestowed on those who survived here. Two large suitcases against the wall by her table, coupled with the steamer trunk that had almost waylaid me near the door, implied she had just arrived from far away, but left me to question why anyone would travel from anywhere else to come here.

She'd busied herself getting the boy settled and thankfully hadn't noticed that I'd been staring at her, but then she looked up and found my eyes. "You rode in with those men in the saloon. Who are they?" she asked and I could hear the same tremor in her voice as I'd heard from the Mexican woman.

"They're deputies, ma'am. They've just caught the most wanted outlaw in California," I answered.

Her face fell, her lips taut. "I see," she said curtly, but her hands, once folded delicately in her lap, were now clutched together in anxiety.

Her tension aroused my instincts. The story I'd just thought at an end could well have acquired new life. "Is there something I can do for you, ma'am," I asked tactfully.

She stared deep into my eyes as if she wanted to see the darkest depths of my soul, searching for a clue to assure her that I would not betray whatever confidence she might choose to disclose. Then she turned abruptly toward her son, her back to me.

Thank you, sir, but no, there is nothing you can do," she snapped. And I realized at once that there was indeed more to this story, and that she knew, whether by instinct or from her careful examination of my inner spirit, the total extent of my inclination to spread her story to the world.

Immediately I felt the warmth as blood rushed to my face. "I apologize, ma'am. I'm a reporter by training. It's my nature to snoop into the private lives of others, but, like young Tommy, my own mother instilled in me a respect for a lady's privacy. I give you my word, I'll divulge nothing you tell me without your express permission and I will give you whatever help I can."

She turned back toward me, a skeptical look in her eyes. But her tightly clasped hands conveyed her need for a friend, a confidant. "Maria," she called to the cook, "is there something Tommy can do outside, maybe in the back? He's getting restless."

"Oh, si, señora. The chickens, they need to eat," Maria said in suddenly reasonably good English.

"Tommy, you know how to feed chickens don't you?"

"You know I do, Ma," Tommy answered.

"Run on back to the kitchen then and let Maria show you what to do."

"Okay, Ma." The boy scurried toward the kitchen then stopped and turned back to his mother. "Aren't we gonna go find my Pa soon?" he asked, and his mother's face instantly blanched white. But she kept her composure. "I'll see," she said in that way mothers have of easing their children's hopes slowly without having to say no right away.

Maria waved. "Come, Tommy, the chickens, they are hungry,"

she urged and Tommy turned toward her, glanced quickly to his Ma, but then followed Maria outside.

I stood. "My name is Benjamin Eades, ma'am. I suspect that I've been in California only a short time longer than you, but if there is anything I can do, I'm at your service."

She sat sideways in her chair, hands again folded in her lap, head lowered. "That is kind of you, Mr. Eades," she began. "I'm Clara Hodges of Tennessee and you are right, I've only just arrived in this place." She spoke in her slow measured manner, all the while without looking in my direction, but then she turned and I felt a surprisingly hot glare from her eyes, much like heat from an open stove. "I was to meet my husband here," she continued. "He wrote and begged me to come as quickly as I could. He'd made a lot of money and bought a ranch. Now we could be together again, like he'd promised."

She looked down once more then dabbed her eyes with a handkerchief she'd held crushed in her palm. Yet she hadn't sounded tearful, or even sad. And to me it seemed as if a bitterness percolated deep beneath her words, not a rage that would boil over like an unwatched pot, but instead more the smoldering indignation of a stew set atop a small flame to simmer slow and long.

I held my tongue, sure she had more to say, unwilling to interrupt the flow of her thoughts, for even now she considered what could best be said and what must remain within her. She'd called herself Clara Hodges, but the man we'd captured, Tom Bell, was her husband. Each mannerism she'd used, every expression she'd made, confirmed it.

She had no trust in me, nor should she, but still she had an immense need for a friend. A change of plans so unimaginable, so shocking, so disastrous had hit her in little more than an instant with all the force of a locomotive at full steam. Isolated here at the end of the earth, a continent away from family and friends, she'd just seen the man she married, the father of her child, drug into a tent saloon by a ragtag posse of vagabond deputies, and then heard him labeled as the most wanted outlaw in California by an equally scruffy stranger. Many women would have broken down under such a burden.

She dropped her hands back to her lap. "What did he do?" she asked quietly.

"A woman was killed—"

"No, I don't want to know," she interjected, her tone as sharp as a barber's blade. Then she frowned. "I'm sorry," she offered, softer now. "Did he kill her?"

"No one knows. Everybody was shooting. It could have been any of the gang. Still, he was the brains. He did the planning. He's responsible."

She stood and turned to the open window. "What will happen to him?" she asked.

"They're going to hang him, ma'am, just as soon as the Stockton stage comes through."

"Oh Lord!" she gasped and her hands flew to her face. "Won't he get a trial?"

"No ma'am. I'm sorry."

"But, that's not—"

"I know, it's not the way things are done back east, but it's how they're done here. He's admitted his crimes, and now he's making his peace with God."

"Oh, poor Tom," she dabbed at her eyes again. "But I'm not surprised. There was always something about him, something different, odd. He's so smart, but so hard to please. Everything always had to be his way. If someone crossed him he would lash out against them, sometimes violently, and yet, at the same time, he had a wonderful generosity. If he liked you he'd give you anything he could. He's a doctor you know, a surgeon and very skilled, but he never was able to dedicate the time necessary for such a demanding profession. He always wanted the easy way."

I shuffled my feet, uncomfortable discussing her soon to be dead husband, but felt I must say something positive about him. "I've heard how he once robbed a rider deep in a canyon, far from anywhere. He took the man's gold and his horse but left him enough food to stay alive until he could reach a town. Another time he shot a miner in the leg as he stole his gold then took the time to tend the wound before fleeing."

"That sounds like Tom," she said and turned to face me. "The place he bought is near here. Maria's husband, Juan, offered to take me there after the Stockton stage arrives, but that was before . . ." Her voice broke and for the first time I sensed her grief.

"We found him on a ranch a few miles up the river." I said. "It didn't look like much, a small adobe house, a barn and a few head of cattle scattered across this empty grassland. Surely you don't plan to go there now,"

"Where did you live before you came to California, Mr. Eades?" she asked.

"Baltimore, ma'am."

"You were raised in a city then?" she continued.

"Well, yes."

"This country may look like empty grassland to you, but to a cow or a horse it's heaven on earth. And to me, it's the only place I have to live. There is no choice."

"Ma'am, you can't run a ranch by yourself, not here. How will you survive?"

"What would you have me do, go to San Francisco and work in a gambling house, or worse?" Indignation dripped from her words and left me at a loss while she continued, "My father raised cattle and bred horses in Tennessee, Mr. Eades. I do have some knowledge of what is involved."

She wore a look of determination and I realized her mind was set. "At least allow me to accompany you there," I offered. "Perhaps I can help get you settled in."

"I would be most grateful, Mr. Eades, but, please, call me

Clara,"

A sudden commotion rumbled in from the rear of the room and Tommy bounced through the back door. "I fed the chickens, Ma. It was fun," he yelled, excited and happy.

She turned to her son. "I'm glad, Tommy," she said with a sudden, unexpected smile then looked to me. "This trip has been so hard on him," she explained.

Maria had followed Tommy inside. "Juan, he is coming with the wagon, señora. The stage to Stockton will be here pronto," she said just as a two-wheeled farm cart pulled by a floppy eared nag rolled up to the front of the café and a short Mexican man in a wide brimmed straw hat jumped down, wrestled the steamer trunk into the back then climbed onto the seat and moved the cart away. The clatter of hooves grew from the south. The Stockton stage was coming at a dead run.

Mrs. Hodges spun toward me, panic in her eyes. "I can't have Tommy see this," she whispered and I knew she referred to what would follow the departure of the stage.

No mother would want her son to see his father hanged, and the stage would only stay long enough for a change of horses and a quick meal, a half hour, maybe less. Then Tom Bell, or Hodges, or whatever his name, would be hauled from the tent and strung up from a nearby tree. I'd seen it happen before. I'd heard their plans. I had no doubts.

"Maria, would Juan object if I borrowed his cart to take Mrs. Hodges to her ranch, I'll return it as soon as I can." I asked. Her dark eyes darted from me to Clara, whose hands were again clenched tightly together, knuckles white, worry etched deep in her face. Across the road three men from the posse lurched out of the saloon, drunk, loud and carrying a rope with a hangman's knot tied on one end. "Madre de Dios," Maria exclaimed. "No, señor, Juan would not mind, but I will tell him for you. You must go quickly, I think. Come."

Clara took Tommy's arm and Maria hustled both of them out

the door. I grabbed my report, the two suitcases and followed. The cart waited just past the end of the building. I threw the bags beside the trunk just as the stage pulled up in front of the adobe amid loud shouts from the driver and weary snorts from the horses. Tommy and his mother were already sitting on the crude cart bench. I climbed up beside her.

"Thank you so much, Maria," Clara said as I snapped the reins. "Vaya con Dios, señora," Maria replied and we rolled slowly toward the river then onto the ferry that waited there for the Stockton stage. As the ferryman pulled on the ropes that inched us across, I looked back to see Juan replacing the stage team with four fresh mustangs while Maria ushered the passengers inside the adobe for their meal.

The flat-nosed boat banged into the far pier and off we rode. Soon the small settlement was hidden behind the trees that flanked the stream. I felt a hand on my leg and knew at once it was Clara. I looked over into eyes as brown as the grass around us.

"Thank you, Ben," she said warmly and it came to me that she was right, this was a good place to raise cattle and horses, and maybe even kids if she was willing.

The End

– John Putnam

Born and raised in a small South Carolina town John went on to graduate from U.C. Berkeley with a degree in music, but found a laptop keyboard more his forte than a piano. He still lives and works in Berkeley and while researching for his blog, MyGoldRushTales.com, he uncovered his love for the excitement and adventure of the California gold rush.

His first four short stories won story of the month in Frontier Tales. John's first novel, *Hangtown Creek*, sets the scene for his second gold country story in which a pretty girl sweeps young Tom Marsh off his feet and when Tom decides to look for her missing pa he quickly finds himself eyeball to eyeball with the deadliest fiend in the gold country. *Into the Face of the Devil,* was published in 2013 by Pen-L Publishing.

THE HOG LOT SHOOTING

by Ellen Gray Massey

Ocie Tulley frowned as she handed the neatly typed and bound manuscript back to the young man who was eagerly awaiting her opinion. "Lies," she said. Behind her steel-rimmed glasses her eyebrows contracted, forming two deep lines in her forehead. "Mostly lies."

Affronted by her unexpected condemnation, he watched as with steady hands, she tied her sunbonnet straps under her chin, the shadows from its stiff brim making her wrinkled face even blacker. Spurning the young man's help, she pulled herself from the chair with her homemade crutch and limped out to the porch of her clapboard cabin. She wiped the perspiration on her face with a flowered handkerchief from her apron pocket and supporting herself with her crutch, stared across the dirt road at her hog lot.

"But..." Grayson's body stiffened at her blatant dismissal of his scholastic research. The presumption of this former school teacher! And after all his efforts to find her, overcome her suspicions of him, and persuade her to read his thesis. When he pointed to her brother's name in his paper, she had stopped shaking her head. Then she opened the screen door to let him into her living room when he explained that he wanted to see the actual rooms in her house where the dead men were carried after the shooting.

Controlling his resentment, he pointed across the dirt road

where she was looking and demanded she agree. "But wasn't over there where young Mort Killion fell over dead?"

"That's where he tumbled off his horse—right over the fence into my hog lot," Ocie said.

"And over there..." his lips tightened into a smug line as he pointed to their right down and across the road about fifty yards to a big white oak tree in the woods pasture, ". . . over east there, isn't that where Pinkerton detective, Oliver Larimore, was mortally wounded by Mort's brother?"

"That's where the last bullet hit him." Ocie nodded her head.

"Then how can you say my account of the gun battle is lies?"

"'Cause them two fellers getting shot is about all you got right." Ocie eased her thin body into a homemade rocker on the porch, smoothing out her apron over her long print dress. Sighing, she rocked with a rhythmic squeak-rumble as the runners of her chair rolled back and forth across the cracks in the unpainted, rough oak floor of the porch.

"That was a long time ago," Grayson said, his frown deepening. He thumbed through the pages of his manuscript. Perhaps you've forgotten."

"A long time, yes," Ocie agreed. "Forty-eight years last March. But I remember." Her eyes did not look at her indignant visitor, but continued to stare across the road.

Grayson sat on the steps, one foot swinging among the golden marigolds as if they and not the woman were opposing him. He looked alternately at his pages, at Ocie, and at the two fatal spots across the road, his eyes squinting in vexed concentration. A Model A breezed down the road followed by a cloud of dust which settled on the hood and canvas top of Grayson's new 1921 Buick touring car. Ocie's hogs grunted and nuzzled one another as they wallowed in the cool mud in the corner of the lot—the very spot where many years ago young Mort Killion finally lost consciousness and fell off his horse after earlier being hit with a bullet from the gun of Pinkerton detective Oliver Larimore.

"And . . ." Grayson insisted, "wasn't Mort Killion's body carried to your house, this one right here?"

Her eyebrows lowered as she nodded and pointed to her bedroom window overlooking the porch. "And laid on my bed, hog manure and all."

Grayson's self-assurance was returning, "Well . . ."

"And Wally's body," Ocie mumbled so softly Grayson could barely hear her. Tears welled up in her black eyes. One tear coursed its way down a wrinkled path to her chin. She wiped it away with her handkerchief. "His body was here, too, laid out on the porch." She tapped the spot beside her with her crutch.

"Yes. Yes, of course, your brother Wally."

"You don't hardly mention him in that story 'cept to say he was a guide for the Pinkertons. Varmints like the Killion brothers and a famous detective from Chicago—that's all you write about." Her mouth tightened as her eyes never left his. "What about my brother? He was killed, too. All you said about him was, 'The Pinkerton's Negro guide was killed in the gunfire.'"

Grayson looked away, his haughty manner softening.

Perhaps I should have talked with you before writing this." Ocie nodded again in time with her rocking. "If you are the historian you claim to be, you sure enough should have. Didn't you wonder why Wally was guiding the detectives? Or why they were all here at his own place? Written history ought to answer such important questions. Ought to have the facts straight."

Grayson threw his shoulders back and raised his head, once again angry that she dared to criticize him—to censure him, a noted authority on guerrilla activities on the Missouri-Kansas border before, during, and after the Civil War. In a voice louder than necessary, as if lecturing to his freshman university class, he blurted, "I have read every word that has ever been written about the gun battle. I read the reports from Pinkerton National Detective Agency, and . . ." he paused to give emphasis to this fact, ". . . and I interviewed Guy Killion himself up there in the penitentiary before he got paroled." He paused to let the magnitude of this sink in.

Ocie grunted as if to say, "So what?"

"Guy Killion was the only surviving witness to the shooting in which his younger brother Mort and the Pinkerton detective Oliver Larimore were killed," Grayson continued. "And he described it to me in great detail."

Though Ocie looked straight at Grayson, her negative expression did not change. "Lies," she said.

Irritated with her attitude, Grayson opened his manuscript. "He drew a map—see here it is. I was impressed with him. He didn't seem a cold-blooded killer. His manner was reserved, but courteous. He told exactly where everyone was and what happened."

She grunted again.

"Hell, woman!" He'd had about enough of her disrespect. Looking from the map to the hog lot and big oak tree across the road, he explained as if to a child, "The map is accurate. Guy had already been caught, tried, convicted, and had about served out his time. Even seemed sorry. Why would he lie, especially since what he said about the event corroborated all the written testimonies?"

"Event?" she snorted at his choice of word.

Ocie pressed her lips tightly together. Her hands clutched the worn arms of the chair as she increased the tempo of her rocking. The gentle squeak-rumble became an ominous crackling, almost like gunshots as the wooden runners slammed across the cracks.

Grayson patted the rust-colored cover of his manuscript defensively. "Yes, this is a carefully researched and documented thesis. Because of its thoroughness, I've been asked to present a reading at the Western Historical Society Annual Meeting next month in Kansas City."

The noise of the rocker stopped—the only sound an occasional squeal from a pig across the road.

Grayson looked up from his manuscript at Ocie. The pinkish palm of her right hand pushed back into the recess of her bonnet a strand of kinky white hair. In the shadow of the bonnet brim, her eyes were soot black and flared in disagreement.

Aghast, Grayson suddenly understood her resentment and guessed what she wasn't telling him. "Guy Killion wasn't the only surviving witness to the shooting?"

Ocie's hands relaxed and her eyes softened as she resumed her gentle rocking motion.

"You saw it all!" Excitement replaced Grayson's irritation. Ocie's eyes rolled at his stupidity.

"Why didn't you say so?" Grayson asked. The researcher in him was eager to learn what she knew. "In all the reports and coverage, the only mention ever made of you was that the wounded detective died here in your house."

Ocie wiped her face again with her handkerchief, but said nothing.

Suspecting her reluctance to speak through fear of retaliation from the other Killion brothers, Grayson said gently, "Didn't you know, Mrs. Tulley, that Guy Killion is dead now?"

Ocie released a barely audible sigh. She shifted in her chair to face him better.

"Yes, he died last month. Guy was the last of the four Killion brothers," Grayson said. "There is no longer any danger from any of them."

Ocie's rocking slowed to an occasional squeak as she studied Grayson's face. Her lips relaxed their thin, tight line, showing their red fullness.

Holding up his manuscript, he said, "Okay, since you say what I've written is lies, then tell me what did happen."

For the first time since his arrival, Ocie smiled, her white false teeth gleaming in her black face, giving her a youthful, pixie-like appearance. With another glance at the hog lot where Mort Killion fell dead, she braked the rocking movement of her chair with her good foot, leaned forward, and looked Grayson in the face. One historian to another, she began her story.

"The last gun battle of the war was right here in March of eighteen and seventy-four. Here in western Missouri the Civil War didn't end in sixty-five like it did everywhere else. The Killions and Jesse and Frank James, and some other Bushwhacker trash like them liked the shooting, killing, stealing, and raping so much that they just kept on. Kept killing northern sympathizers and helping themselves to anything they wanted— even robbing banks and trains. And what local law there was couldn't, or wouldn't, do much about it.

"My brother and I were born slaves. After the war we saved enough for the down-payment on this forty acres here. Some of our relatives had farms near us—lots of coloreds in the neighborhood. We farmed, mostly raising and butchering hogs like I still do, but to get cash to meet our yearly mortgage payments, Wally worked some at the docks on the Osage at River Bend when there was enough water that steamboats could travel that far upstream. Other times he took what jobs he could find in town— like guiding cattle buyers.

"Before I started teaching school, I worked some at the hotel. Coloreds didn't make as much as the whites, but the community of us former slaves here in this neighborhood then, we helped one another. Whites and coloreds together, we got along.

"The Killion brothers were often in this vicinity 'cause they had lots of sympathy among the white folks here. Some of the colored, too. The Killions were sort of heroes because they were part of the gang that burned out Lawrence, Kansas, in sixty-three after the Kansas Jayhawkers burned down River Bend two years earlier.

"Well anyways, the Killions would hole up around here in between jobs in this rough hilly country. Along the bends in the river there were lots of good hiding places and good bluff lookouts. People hid them. The sheriff and other lawmen could never catch them."

Ocie's eyes narrowed and her lips tightened. The pitch of her voice raised as she talked.

"But they didn't get sympathy from you?" Grayson asked.

She shook her head vigorously. "They thought they did. They'd stop here—we're right on the road, you know—and make me fix them a meal. They'd carry away with them anything they wanted. Wally had to rub down their horses and feed them. They never paid anything. Just thought it was due them—treated us like slaves again, ordered us around, and threatened to shoot us if we ever told the sheriff about them. Would have, too. We did what they wanted. We had to put up with all kinds of people in order to survive."

"It was a terrible time," Grayson agreed.

"The four brothers would ride in pairs. Never all together. If something happened to one pair, the other retaliated." Pinpoints of hate came into Ocie's eyes.

"Did they ever . . ." Grayson hesitated, wondering how to ask about the worst of all crimes against women.

"Yes," Ocie said. "That stinking, red-headed Mort Killion . . ."

She clenched her gnarly fists as if strangling the outlaw. "Mort Killion came by time after time. The others would stand by and laugh, make vulgar jokes. Called me pig and lots of other words I won't say. To them I was no better than those hogs across the road. Only afterwards I could cook for them."

"So what did you do?"

The sympathy in Grayson's eyes encouraged her. "Wally and me, we figured out a plan to trap them."

"Tell me," Grayson said, leaning forward to catch every word.

"As long as the Killions just preyed on ordinary folks not much was done to catch them. But when they started to robbing banks and trains, then not only the local sheriff, but hot-shot detectives hired by the railroad came looking for them.

"One day in March of seventy-four, two city fellers checked

into the hotel while I was working. They said they were cattle
buyers and asked around if anyone had cattle to sell. Now Wally
and me thought they were too well armed to be cattle buyers.
They didn't carry the regular Smith and Wesson rifles or Colt
pistols like most of the local men did. Wally said that they had an
English-made gun called the Trantor, a .43 caliber with a 5 7/8
inch barrel. I know guns. I remembered.

"Now the guns aroused suspicions that these fellers might be
lawmen, especially since there had been another railroad robbery
north of River Bend a few weeks before. Talk was that the Killions
did it. The sheriff had been around earlier asking everyone about
them. But he quit looking after a few days.

"The cattle buyers hung around the bars and on the square
listening to the gossip, we thought, hoping to get some information about the Killions. So we figured this was our chance.
When the cattle buyers, one was Oliver Larimore—I forget the
other—when they asked for a guide to show them where they
could find some cattle to buy, Wally took the job. They planned
on leaving the next morning.

"I pretended to be sick so I wouldn't have to go to work at the
hotel. The timing was right, for we knew that two of the Killion
brothers, Mort and Guy, were staying the night with the O'Connors,
some folks catty-cornered across the section from us.

We didn't know whether they would stay there for noon
dinner the next day or come to our place as they often did. But
we knew they would stop by sometime during the day. I stayed
home so when they came, I could keep them here until Wally
maneuvered the detectives to capture them.

"The road leading to the farm where they could buy the cattle
went right by the O'Connor place. To check out the house,
Detective Larimore went to the door pretending to get directions
and to ask if they had any cattle to sell, while Wally and the other
feller waited out in the road on their horses. Larimore chatted
pleasantly a few minutes, learning that O'Connor had no cattle

but a woman down the road did. O'Connor gave him directions to her house—the same woman that Wally was taking them to.

"While there, Larimore looked around for any trace of the Killions. O'Connor was nervous and seemed to want him to leave quickly. Though Larimore's trained eye didn't see any evidence that the brothers were there, he believed from O'Connor's manner that they were close.

"Meanwhile the other detective glanced around outside the best he could without causing suspicions. He noticed that there were more horse tracks in the dirt than one family would make, but he decided that if the tracks belonged to the outlaws, they had already left because many of them headed north."

Grayson interrupted. "How do you know all these details? Those men were all killed, and you were here at the time." Ocie gave her pixie-like grin. "Yes, I was here, right on this porch almost where you are now, listening and watching for the horses."

"Then you couldn't know what they saw at the O'Connors. You're making all this up."

Shaking her head, Ocie held up her hand for him to be patient.

"Well, the Killions were at the O'Connor place all along, even though the detective fellers didn't know it. The outlaws heard the horsemen coming down the road and climbed to the attic where they could see the room below as well as outside. They knew how to keep out of sight. They had already hidden their horses back in the timber behind the house.

"I can't believe that those detectives didn't suspect anything. I'm sure Wally did. Then they did another dumb thing. O'Connor told later that the Killions watched them leave. But instead of going straight north on the main road to the woman with the cattle, Larimore led them northwest on an old trail that cut across to our house.

"Wally tried to get him back on the main road. Now even though Wally knew the men were not cattle buyers, the men didn't know that he knew this, so Wally could only object, and then go along with them. Wally didn't tell them of our plan— wouldn't have paid any attention to him anyways for white folks think we are stupid. He intended to tell them when he saw that the Killions were in our house.

"Our plan was simple. When the brothers arrived, I would feed them as always in the kitchen where you can't see the road. While they were eating, I'd get their guns, or at least maneuver them so that their guns were not handy. Then Wally and the detectives could surround the place and capture them.

"But, for this to work, Wally needed to keep the detectives away long enough to give the Killions time to get here. Going down the road a piece to ask about the cattle would do that. Then while the detectives would haggle with the woman over the sale, Wally could watch and listen for the Killions to leave O'Connor's house and ride to our place. Wally probably saw something at O'Connor's that told him the Killions were still there. But Lari- more's cutting across and getting to our house first ruined our plan, so Wally could only go along with them, playing dumb.

"Meanwhile back at O'Connor's, Mort Killion was convinced that the heavily armed strangers were detectives when they didn't follow O'Connor's directions to the cattle. Rather than let the them go on their way, he convinced his more cautious brother to chase after them.

"I'll get rid of the son-of-bitches," he bragged to O'Connor. "Think they can fool me!"

"Here at home, I was about to decide that we missed them, when instead from the east road where I was watching for riders, I heard horses coming on the old trail across the field from behind.

"This trail didn't follow the straight section line north and then turn west as the road did, but cut across the northeast corner of the section through the fields and over a woody patch to join the road by our orchard. I heard the slowly moving horses before I saw them emerge from the timber.

"At first I thought they were the Killions, who sometimes took that trail. I was excited, but trembly all over, thinking that our trap was working. Then my heart gave a skip when I recognized Wally's roan pull ahead of the other two to the road in front of our house where he knew I'd be watching. He stopped by the hog shed. We signaled each other that we hadn't seen the Killions. He also waved me back into the house. We both knew this was trouble.

"I watched the two Pinkerton men cautiously ride up, guns out and ready, ready for the outlaws. Larimore on a bay mare was in the rear. Seeing everything was quiet, they joined Wally who waved them on. The first detective reached the hog lot just as we heard horsemen galloping up the trail.

"I grabbed the rifle from under my bed and crouched in the front room under this window that overlooks the porch and out across the road to the hog lot.

"Mort Killion, his face as red as his hair stringing from under his hat, was carrying a double-barreled shotgun. Guy, more cautious with his head turning in all directions, had one pistol drawn and another in plain sight in his gun belt. Hearing the hoofbeats, the first Pinkerton man spurred his horse west down the road and disappeared around the bend. No one around here ever heard of him since that day.

"Pointing his gun alternately at Wally and Larimore and backed up by Guy's gun, Mort Killion yelled out as he rode up to them, 'Drop yer guns, damnit.'

"Wally let go of his like it was burning hot. Larimore swore, but dropped his, also.

"Wally cried out, 'Mort, it's me, Wally. These here fellers are only cattle buyers from the city. They jest this morning hired me to guide 'em.'

"Guy was behind his brother. Alert, his eyes now watching Wally and Larimore, Guy dismounted slowly, dropping his reins to the ground. His gelding stood quiet in the middle of the road. Without taking his eyes off of Larimore and Wally, he pocketed Wally's pistol and then picked up Larimore's fancy English gun.

"'You're in bad company, boy,' Guy said to Wally. 'This here feller looks like a detective to me.' He studied Larimore's gun, pushing up the brim of his hat to see it better. 'This ain't no cattle buyer's gun.'

"'Aw, Guy, a man's got to carry a good gun. You know with all the killin' and robbin' 'round here you've got to have good guns to protect yourself,' Wally said.

"Poised like an animal ready to pounce at any second, Mort glared through the sights of his gun at Larimore. Larimore knew his danger, but sat very still watching Mort closely. The gun battle began while Guy was momentarily distracted talking with Wally. Mort squeezed the trigger just a fraction of a second before Larimore shot Mort with a number two Smith and Wesson he pulled from his gray coat.

"Both men were wounded. Mort's shot stuck Larimore in the right shoulder. Larimore's bullet went through Mort's shoulder near his collar bone. The red blood that spread over his coat was brighter than his hair that almost covered the wound.

"Larimore's bay mare reared at the shot. Guy's horse that was only ground-tied ran off, bucking and neighing in fright. "Guy swirled around, crouched, and shot at Larimore. His bullet went high.

"With his left hand, Larimore neck-reined his excited mare up the road east and quickly cut off north into the woods for protection. Standing in the stirrups and turning back to fire again, he didn't see the low-hanging limb which caught him across his side just under his shoulder wound. As his horse galloped on, he fell to the ground, his gun flying a good twelve feet away and clattering on some rocks. Larimore didn't move—just a gray bump in the leaves and mosses under the white oak tree.

"Though bleeding, Mort spurred his horse after Larimore.

Weaving from side to side, his long hair falling into his face, he held on to the saddle horn with one hand to keep his seat. Cursing and yelling, he pulled up short when he reached the fallen detective. Seeing that he didn't move, Mort fired two careless shots into Larimore's sprawled body. Then he reined his horse back toward Guy who was still standing in the road with his gun pointed at Wally.

"Wally was crying, 'I don't know nothin' about detectives, Guy. I was jest . . .'

"This was when Mort stopped at the hog lot fence. He steadied himself in the saddle. He leveled his gun and shot once, turned swiftly around in his saddle and shot again. There was a third shot almost at the same time as Mort's second shot. Like a sack of corn that had been dangling from the saddle horn, Mort Killion dropped dead from the saddle, toppling over the rail fence into our hog lot."

Ocie paused, her chin resting on her chest. Her bonnet completely hid her face.

Grayson said nothing for a few seconds. When Ocie lifted her head, her face was wet. This time she let the tears drop unwiped from her chin.

"And your brother?" Grayson asked gently. "It was him that Mort shot just before he fell?"

With one brief nod, she tapped the fingers of her right hand on chair arm as she continued.

"I'm sorry, but it's been a while since I thought of poor Wally there in the road. Give me just a minute, please." Ocie closed her eyes and took a breath to steady herself.

Ocie gathered herself and looked up at Grayson. "There's more, but I have to back up a bit. Remember, Guy was on the ground picking up the guns and talking to Wally when the shooting began. Guy's first shot at Larimore missed him, but, being the cool-headed one, he kept his gun sighted on Larimore's back as the detective fled. Guy couldn't fire again for fear of hitting his brother.

"During this, Wally was still sitting there in the road on his roan. Too late to run like the other detective did. He couldn't outrun Guy's bullet, and besides, Wally wasn't their enemy. The detective was. If he sat still, Wally wasn't worried about Guy. But Mort? A different matter. Both Wally and I kept our eyes on him, hoping he would fall from his wound.

"Mort was wild and swearing savagely when he returned from chasing and putting those two extra shots into Larimore's body. Mort paused at the hog lot fence. He steadied himself in the saddle and deliberately pointed his big navy pistol at Wally. He murdered him—shot him through the neck. Wally dropped to the ground almost at Guy's feet.

"Immediately, almost with the same motion, noticing a slight movement from Larimore like he was after his gun, Mort fired one last time in Larimore's direction. Just as he made that wild shot, a bullet knocked him off his horse.

"There were three bodies on the ground now—Wally in the road, Mort in the hog lot, and Larimore under the oak tree. Only Guy was left.

"When Wally fell, Guy booted him over to make sure he was dead. Kicked my brother just like he was a thieving coyote! Guy swore something I couldn't hear and then ran to the lot where Mort fell. Pushing the hogs out of his way, he waded into the mire of the pen, and knelt to see that his brother was truly dead. He removed Mort's watch and pistols and rummaged through his pockets for other personal belongings. Seething with rage and looking all about, he then glared at our house, straight to the window where I was crouched."

Ocie's voice broke so that she had to stop talking.

Grayson stared at her in amazement. "You were the one that killed Mort Killion, not Oliver Larimore!"

Ocie nodded. "Larimore's pistol shot at the beginning of the shooting wounded Mort, but my bullet finished him. It was what knocked him over the fence into the hog pen."

"Did Guy see you?"

"No."

"Hear the shot?"

"It was at almost the same time Mort fired at Larimore. Hard to distinguish."

"But you don't know for sure he didn't hear it?" Grayson asked.

"No."

"And you've lived all these years afraid that Guy would some-day . . ." Grayson didn't finish. He dropped his manuscript in admiration.

Ocie resumed her quiet rocking. Her whole body seemed to be agreeing as it rocked forward and backward.

"You could have shot Guy also. Why didn't you?"

"He didn't shoot my brother. Could have, but didn't. Mort was the mean one."

"In my interview with Guy in prison, he didn't tell it like this. He said Larimore shot first. He bragged about how Mort, though mortally wounded with Larimore's bullet, did all that riding and shooting until he finally keeled over. That was the way he said it happened."

"Larimore's bullet only hit his shoulder. Mine went through his heart."

"But why did Guy look toward the house if he didn't see you?" Ocie shrugged her shoulders. "'Course he wouldn't tell the story the way it really happened. Couldn't let anyone know that a colored person killed the notorious Mort Killion—and a woman at that. More fitting end to be killed by a Pinkerton man in a gun battle."

Grayson's respect increased. "And here you've outlived them all."

"Probably."

"What do you mean, probably?" Just when he thought he had

the complete story, Ocie kept giving new hints. "Except you, everyone involved in that gun battle is dead now that Guy has died."

"Maybe not." Ocie's stubborn stance indicated there was more to her story.

"How's that possible?"

"The shooting brought the neighbors running right quick. I stashed my rifle back under my bed, and sneaking out the back, I swung around to the front when the others got there, just like I'd been working in the garden and just heard the shots. Guy was stomping around in a violent temper, giving orders to carry Mort's body into my house. He ordered the O'Connor boy to stand guard over him. 'I'll come back and shoot you if anyone harms his body,' he said.

"Guy would have too, even though the O'Connors were friends. Didn't his brother just kill Wally who was his friend? Guy wanted to make sure no one would molest the body, like cut off his head or string him up.

"Then before the sheriff could get there, Guy rode Mort's horse south to Arkansas to join his two other brothers.

"The neighbors that came were concerned with caring for Larimore, for he wasn't dead, though he had Mort's three bullets in him. The men carried him onto Wally's bed.

"And Wally? No one paid any attention to him, for they were either scared of Guy, working on Larimore, or were busy running to River Bend after the sheriff and doctor. Poor Wally was of no consequence. 'Cept to me.

"I grabbed an old quilt, spread it in the dirt beside him there in the road, and rolled him over on to it. Then I wrapped it around him and dragged him to the porch. By lifting his head and shoulders and then his legs, I managed to get him out of the sun up on the porch.

"Just when I had him stretched out and was putting pebbles on his eyes to keep them closed, Guy Killion stomped out of the house after seeing to Mort's body. His angry eyes held mine for several seconds like he was trying to decide what to do. Without saying a word, he jumped off the porch, climbed on his horse, and galloped off. I never saw him again. Or either of his two surviving brothers."

"You still haven't explained. You and Guy were the only survivors of the battle. Now, since Guy's death, you are the only one left. For sure Guy didn't tell you what happened at the O'Connors, so how did you know?"

"Oliver Larimore told me."

"But he was in a coma until he died the next day. The sheriff and the doctor both testified to that."

"More lies," Ocie said.

Grayson knew he had to let Ocie tell her story in her own way. "Then . . ."

"It didn't take the sheriff and his deputies long to make the two miles from town. They were here not fifteen minutes after Guy left. The sheriff left one man to guard Larimore while the rest followed Guy's trail. Never caught up with him, though. "The doctor arrived soon after. Even though I was trying to prepare Wally's body for burial, the doctor grabbed me to help with Larimore. The doctor dug out three bullets, just like your account says, but they weren't where you said. One was in his right shoulder, one in his thigh, and the other hit his hand—not all in his chest as you wrote in those papers.

"Now that Oliver Larimore was no dummy. He pretended to be dead or in a coma so the Killions would leave him alone. But he wasn't dead, though he was bad off. The doctor fixed him up that evening, telling me what to do and promising to come back in the morning.

"By this time there was a crowd of people out here—not just the neighbors, but people from town and miles away. Ignoring me like I didn't exist, they helped themselves to any food they could find in my kitchen. They raided the cellar and smoke house, and even milked the cow for her milk. You'd have thought

my house was main street in front of the court house the way
everybody tramped through it, viewing Mort Killion's body and
everyone telling everyone else what happened. 'Course none of
them knew.

"Old Mr. O'Connor was the loudest. He told his story over and
over to each newcomer how the Killion brothers forced him to
put them up the night before, and about the cattle-buying strangers stopping. He boasted that he knew right away that they were
Pinkerton detectives. He'd look through the door at Larimore's
unconscious body lying in Wally's bed and brag, 'Yup, soon as I
seen this here feller I knowed he was a detective. 'Course, I didn't
tell the Killions that.'

"Stories got magnified as they were told. Instead of the eight
shots actually fired, the talk made at least twenty. How with a
bullet from a Pinkerton Trantor in his heart, Mort Killion did all
that riding and straight shooting. He became a sort of hero right
there.

"I didn't think I could stand it. Here was my own murdered
brother lying out on the porch almost at their feet, but they paid
no more mind to him than if he'd been one of our hogs that got
shot with a stray bullet.

"As the doctor stepped out on the porch after finishing with
Larimore, he shook his head and told the crowd milling around,
'Pretty bad shape. Don't think he'll last the night.'

Then he ordered me, 'Go tend to him.'

"When I laid my hand on his forehead to check his fever,
Larimore whispered to me, 'I'm all right for now. Go see about
your brother.' Then he closed his eyes again as he lost consciousness.

"That was the first human act I'd seen all afternoon. Here he
was on his deathbed, and ever since the first shot from Mort
Killion's gun plowed into him at the beginning of the gun battle,
the only words Larimore spoke were concern for me.

"My relatives and me, we buried Wally that evening. We buried him quick 'cause we feared with so many white strangers around that the crowd might turn ugly.

"Even during the night my house and yard was full of men. Several men took turns guarding Mort's body. Thought it an honor. Think of the tales they would tell the rest of their lives about the famous Bushwhacker. The deputy propped himself in a chair right outside Wally's bedroom where Larimore lay, for he feared one of the Killion brothers might come back to finish what they started.

"I stayed beside Larimore the whole night. It was the safest place to be with the deputy guarding the room. Also, I didn't trust anyone else to see to Larimore. I did what the doctor told me and some other things that I knew to do. My mother was a healer and I knew lots of cures. So I tended him.

"He roused several times during the night. Careful not to let anyone else see that he was awake, he smiled his thanks and mumbled a few words. I couldn't make out all he said. 'My fault about your brother.' 'Shouldn't have . . .' 'You saved my life.'

"At first I thought he was saying that my nursing him saved his life, but when he added, 'Good shot,' and 'Have finished me if you hadn't . . .' that I knew my nursing him wasn't what he meant at all.

"The medicine the doctor gave him dulled his pain so that he could sleep for short periods. In between he'd ramble, worried about my danger from the Killions and how his wife would manage if he died. He worried about the baby they were expecting. He'd grab my hand, confusing me with his wife.

"Toward morning his fever broke. His eyes were clear, his mind rational. We talked freely as everyone else in the house was asleep.

"'You're still in lots of danger,' I told him as I removed the bloody bandage from his thigh wound.

"He nodded that he knew that. 'But not from the wounds?'

"I shook my head. We both knew where the danger was.

'Everyone thinks that you killed Mort Killion.'

"He nodded again. 'Good. That's how it should be.'

"'As soon as the other Killions hear that you shot their brother, they will join Guy to hunt you down no matter where you go. They operate as far as Chicago.'"

"'I know.'"

"We needed a plan. Though my plan to trap the Killions cost me my brother, I knew that Larimore's survival, and mine, depended on our coming up with some scheme. This time we had to work together to out-wit them. Too late I realized that Wally and I could have shared our plan with Larimore. He'd have listened.

"'The doctor told everyone that you won't last the night,' I said. 'But you're not that bad.'

"As I put on the fresh dressing and wrapped his thigh with strips torn from my sheets, he caught my hand, held it a moment, and gave it a squeeze of gratitude. He studied my face like he wanted to memorize it.

"I mulled over the problem of the Killions for a few minutes, planning how to keep Larimore safe. 'You've been in a coma ever since you were brought in here and . . .'

"'Most of the time I've been faking that,' he interrupted.

"'That's what I figured.'

"Right then I knew the idea I'd been hatching might work. I glanced around to make sure nobody was awake and whispered, 'Now let's fake your death.'

"Larimore grinned. 'Can we carry it off?'

"'If you're up to it, we can put you in a coffin and cart you out of here to the railroad and ship you back to Chicago.'

"'I'm ready.'

"'I'll put a crowbar under you, and when the train gets underway, you can pry off the lid, get out, and hammer the lid back on.'

"'And my wife . . .' He smiled as he thought of her. 'She could have a funeral for me in Chicago and bury the empty coffin?'

"'Exactly. The Killions will never bother you.'

"We discussed the idea, carefully working out all the details so that no one would ever suspect he didn't die from the gunshot wounds like the doctor predicted."

Grayson's astonishment increased as Ocie talked. "And your plan worked?"

"Yes." The squeak-rumble of Ocie's rocker started again.

"Did he get safely back to Chicago?"

"Yes." Ocie's body was relaxed, her face beautiful in its new peace.

"How do you know?"

"I got a card. Want to see it?"

Grayson jumped up in his excitement. His manuscript spilled unnoticed down the porch steps and landed among the marigolds. "You bet!" This was documented proof of Ocie's story.

Ocie grasped her crutch to stand up. Grayson stepped over to help her. "I can do it, young man," she scolded him, and then laid her hand gently on his arm, patting him in apology for her rudeness. "Sorry, young feller, I guess I'm too independent, but I've been alone for a long time."

Letting the screen door slam behind her, she disappeared into her house. Before Grayson thought it possible, she was back again, pushing her bonnet off her head so that it dangled from its straps down her back. He could clearly see her elfish grin as she handed him a faded and worn penny postcard.

Handling it reverently, he read Ocie's name and address and noted the postmark and date, "Chicago, Illinois, May 12, 1874." He turned the card over and read aloud the unsigned note.

"Our baby boy's name is Wally."

The End

– Ellen Gray Massey

born at Nevada, Missouri, has lived in Laclede County, Missouri, since 1946 and taught for forty-two years in elementary and high schools, and as adjunct faculty for Drury University's Graduate Education Program. She has taught Road Scholar (formerly Elderhostel) classes for the YMCA of the Ozarks at, and for Ozark Adventures in Branson. A prolific speaker and writer, she promotes the Ozarks tirelessly. Since 1990 she has given over 400 talks about the Ozarks and about writing. She was teacher/advisor from 1973-1983 of *Bittersweet, the Ozark Quarterly*, published by her students at Lebanon High School and has done other editorial work professionally and for friends.

Ellen has published numerous articles, short stories, essays, a musical play, as well as 17 novels and 12 non-fiction books. In 1995 she was inducted into the first Writers Hall of Fame of America. She has received 25 awards from the Missouri Writers Guild and three times finalist in Western Writers of America's Golden Spur Awards.

Her recent non-fiction books are *Footprints in the Ozarks: a Memoir* and *Our Robin Is Read: Voices from The Wayside* by

Goldminds Publishing. Recent novels are *Brothers, Blue and Gray and Her Enemies, Blue and Gray* by Gold-minds Publishing, *Skeleton in the Cistern* in Kindle, and *Papa's Gold* by Pen-L Publishing.

Her website is www.ellengraymassey.com

We Won't Tell. Ever.

by Ellen Gray Massey

I'd have never figured it out about Rudy if it hadn't been for that quilt. Well, I guess I should say me and Betsy'd never figured it out. Betsy is my twin sister. She's smart. Sometimes I think she's smarter'n me, but I'd never say it out loud. Probably because she was born five minutes before me. It just takes me a bit to catch up to her. Anyways, me and Betsy figured it out. We are the only ones that know, except Rudy and old Mr. and Mrs. Pendleton. They know, of course. But we won't tell. Ever.

It was summer and Ma had one of her quilting parties. Us kids really looked forward to them. They was always held at our house because we had a big parlor. It was big enough for the ladies to sit around the quilt that was all spread out and sewed into the cloth strips tacked onto the frame. Ever so often the neighbor women (and their kids) come to our house for the day to finish up someone's quilt. One of the ladies would have a quilt already sewed together into some fancy pattern.

Then first thing in the morning on the quilting day, Ma and a couple of women who came early to help her would put the quilt in the frame. They'd set the wooden frame that Pa made on the backs of straight chairs. Then they'd first tack on the lining and then spread out the cotton filling before stretching the pretty pieced top across it all. The women'd all sit around it sewing away all day seeing who could put in the tiniest stitches that held it all together. Being a girl Betsy knows all about that. I know it, too, just like she knows all about man stuff because of me. We know everything together, don't matter that she's a girl and me a boy.

Sometimes there'd be fifteen or twenty ladies there. And talk! They really talk up a storm. I guess it is just as much fun for them as for me and Betsy when they get together like that for all day and still make something useful. And warm and pretty.

One reason me and Betsy like quilting day so much is because Rudy comes with nothing to do all day but be with us. Or he always came before that last gathering. But no more. I guess all three of us grew up some that day.

Well, I'll get to all that directly, but I need to tell you how much we like Rudy. We looked up to him like a big brother, or a best friend. Only he wasn't. Nothing like that. He was old lady Ward's driver.

Me and Betsy just had our twelfth birthday and was feeling kinda superior to the mob of little kids running around playing tag and king on the mountain. But it being mid-summer, there wasn't much work to do on the farm, so Pa give us the day off. He said he wouldn't get a lick of work out of us nohow with all the goings on with the quilting party.

So we spent the day with Rudy. As usual, he was lots of fun. Oh, did I tell you that he is a slave? Well he is. That means in Missouri that he is property not a real person.

Rudy belongs to Mrs. Ward who lives in town —about five miles up the river from our farm. Now there aren't many slaves in our part of the state. The land in the Ozark hills isn't good for crops. Too rocky and hilly. The only good soil is a few acres in the river bottoms, like ours. Just enough ground for Pa and me to raise some corn and hay for our cows, horses, hogs, and Ma's chickens. Nothing like the rich land near the Mississippi and Missouri Rivers where there are big plantations of cotton, hemp, and corn. But even so, some richer people, like the Wards, have a few house slaves like Rudy. He does, or rather he used to do, handiwork around the house. He takes care of the horses and drives their buggy.

He'd usually bring Mrs. Ward to the quilting party early, let her off at the house, and then most times, Mrs. Ward would send him down the main road to the bridge across the river to pick up Mrs. Pendleton. Now the old lady didn't usually have no way to come, her man being so busy and often gone much of the time to Kansas on business. So Rudy'd go get her.

This last time I'm telling about, me and Betsy was waiting for Rudy, for he'd always let us ride with him in the Ward's fancy buggy pulled by that slick, high-stepping mare. When we got to the Pendleton place, Mrs. Pendleton was at the kitchen door and waved at us.

"Come right in, young'uns," she said smiling at us. "You come in too, Rudy," she said to him just like he was somebody. He was kinda surprised at her asking him inside. She motioned him to come and sort of pulled him through the kitchen door. "Here, Rudy, sit down here at the table with the twins and eat some of these cookies while I go get my basket." She had him walk clear across the kitchen and sit there instead of in a chair by the door. Then she went into the bedroom off the kitchen. She kept talking as she went as if she was wanting us to watch her.

Rudy wasn't the only one that was surprised at her unusual actions. Everything she done that morning seemed crazy. I looked at Betsy and she sort of frowned and shock her head as if she couldn't figure it out either. First off I wondered why Mrs. Pendleton had to go get her basket, when she was already to go, waiting for us at the door. I decided maybe she's just forgetful, like my grandpa gets sometimes.

But what about how strange she acted toward Rudy? Nobody invites slaves to sit down at their tables like that. I mean no grownups do 'Course, me and Betsy treat him like anyone else. Always had. We can't understand why not. Rudy is handsome, neat, smart, and one of the nicest people we know.

Betsy wonders more about the difference between colored and whites than I do. She's always trying to figure things out. I don't think about it none. For me that is just the way things are, so why worry. After all this is 1858. Things are as modern as they can be with telegraphs sending messages for hundreds of miles through wires and railroads carrying people anywhere they want to go. I guess I figure slavery has been around so long that it is natural. You're born to it, like you're born to your ma and pa and have to do what they say.

But Betsy isn't so sure. She says that when we get bigger we don't have to do what our folks say and we can leave them if we want to. But slaves can't never leave or do anything they want to do even when they get old. I sometimes think about that, and you know, that isn't right. But there's nothing I can do about it. Anyway that morning of the quilting party, when Mrs. Pendleton was nice to Rudy, Betsy was glad. So was I, even though it was strange.

Rudy grinned real big, especially when he saw the big sugar cookies with fancy red icing decorating the tops. Even though he was sixteen years old, he liked treats as good as me and Betsy did.

Then I saw something that really made me wonder what was going on. Or Betsy saw it and kicked me under the table and pointed for me to notice. As I said, Mrs. Pendleton went into the bedroom just off the kitchen. I thought she was going after her basket, but she left the door open where all of us if we looked could see what she was doing. But she especially looked at Rudy, sort of willing him to notice her. She took a colorful quilt off a shelf and spread it out on the bed, like she hadn't finishing making the bed. She turned to look at Rudy to see if he saw her and then came back into the kitchen and shut the bedroom door.

But what puzzled me more than her actions was what Rudy did. This time I kicked Betsy to look. She was so interested in watching Mrs. Pendleton she didn't notice Rudy. His arm stopped with his cookie half way to his mouth, and he stared wide-eyed for just a second. Then he crammed the cookie in his mouth and almost gagged while swallowing it. He never gobbled his food like that. He often teased me and Betsy about our bad table manners. He taught us how ladies and gentlemen ate.

"All ready to go?" Mrs. Pendleton asked Rudy when she passed him. She was carrying her basket of sewing things. "Come along, Twins," she said to me and Betsy, "we don't want to get Rudy in trouble for being late, now do we?" She held the platter of cookies out, looking at Rudy. "Here, take some more."

We all laughed and ran to the buggy. Rudy looked hard at Mrs. Pendleton before he held her arm to help her climb up to the seat. Me and Betsy jumped in to stand behind them, there not being enough room on the seat for all of us.

"I hear that you'll be leaving us, Rudy," she said in a low voice that she thought we didn't hear. One thing me and Betsy were good at was listening when we weren't supposed to be. We heard all she said even above the mare's shoes striking on the rocky drive and the buggy creaking as it bumped over the rough ground.

"Yes, ma'am," was all Rudy said. I thought he was sort of glum this morning, but I hadn't paid much attention to it. I get glum sometimes too. Being behind him, I couldn't see his face.

"I hear tell that the Wards have sold you to a couple they know in Independence," she continued still talking soft-like. She put her hand on his leg.

"Yes, ma'am, that's what they're planning to do." Rudy kept his face forward trying not to show any emotion. I did see that he gripped the reins really tight, and the veins in his neck sort of moved as he clamped his teeth together.

Now you can imagine what me and Betsy thought. Of course, we knew that slaves were bought and sold, sort of like cattle. It happened all the time. But not to our friends! Betsy gripped my hand hard. She had tears in her eyes, but we didn't say nothing. What could we say? We weren't even supposed to hear them talking.

"Well, I'm here for you," Mrs. Pendleton said and patted his shoulder. She looked a long time into his eyes as if she was trying to get her thoughts to him without talking. He must have got some message, for he nodded, very sad like.

After he drove out of the Pendleton's drive, Rudy started to turn right, down the road and around the bluff and across the bridge like we came.

"No," Mrs. Pendleton said, pointing left. "Let's go down the field and cross the river at the ford. It's much closer."

"But the water's pretty high yet from that rain yesterday," I said. "Pa told us not to ford it."

"It's all right," she said. "We're late. Let's hurry."

She was right. We did get across the river okay, but it was exciting to see the water swirling up on the wheels below us. I'd never crossed when the water was up that high before. But to be on the safe side before urging the mare across, she told Rudy to get down out of the buggy to look closer.

"Walk up and down the bank and gravel bar to be sure it's safe," she said.

"It's fine," Rudy said when he climbed back into the buggy. "The water is falling."

When we got back to our house, Mrs. Pendleton jumped down without waiting for Rudy to help her. We could see into the parlor through the open windows and doors that the women were already working all around the outside borders of the quilt. "Don't forget us," she said to Rudy just before she went into the house with the other ladies and found an empty place. I'd almost forgot that Rudy was going to be sold until she said that. Betsy looked at me with her sad eyes. We almost cried to think of Rudy being sold off like that.

But Rudy put the mare in the barn and during the day acted as if nothing was wrong.

I didn't know what to say to him, but Betsy jumped right in

trying to talk to him. "It that true," she asked.

"Is what true?"

"About the Wards going to sell you?"

"A slave is always for sale," he said, "if the right price comes along."

"But, Rudy, does that mean--"

"Nothing," he said. "It means nothing. Won't happen. I won't be sold." Though his words tried to pretend it was nothing, I thought he seemed awful serious.

His words stumped us for a minute. "But what did Mrs. Pendleton mean when she said, 'Don't forget us'?" I asked.

"Don't forget to take her home."

"Oh!" Betsy looked at me. We both grinned that the news wasn't true. We soon forgot it.

The day went like other quilting parties. We went fishing on the bank by the field. We were all over the field and river, even up to the caves. We climbed over rocks and followed Rudy as he crossed the river on logs washed down by the high water. The river was even lower than it had been that morning. Back at the house, we played games with the other kids. We ate the good dinner the ladies brought. The day went fast and just before chore time the ladies put up their thimbles and needles and thread and started home. Some walked. Some sons or husbands came after them in their farm wagons. A few had come horse-back.

Late in the afternoon old man Pendleton came for his wife so Rudy didn't have to take her home. I didn't see Rudy and Mrs. Pendleton say a word to each other the whole day, but I noticed the Pendletons took the long way home across the bridge, not over the ford. Everyone left, the last lady folded up the finished quilt to take home. Then Ma had me and Betsy put away the quilting frame and straightened up the room.

Next morning while we were feeding the chickens, we heard a couple of hounds baying at the river. The dogs were all excited and pulling on their handler's leashes as they run up the bottom field to our house. You'd a-thought our house was on fire they way they ran.

"What's all the excitement," Pa asked. He just come out of the barn with the full milk bucket in his hand. Me and Betsy were right beside him. He gave the bucket to Betsy, but she stayed to hear what all the ruckus was about.

"Runaway slave," the man said and ran on past us to the house, almost dragged by the speed of the barking dog.

Another hound and its handler ran by. I recognized a sheriff's deputy. "That house boy of the Wards," the second man yelled back.

Betsy looked at me. I could see she was about to drop the bucket of milk. I jumped beside her to help her hold it. She grabbed my arm.

"Ran away sometime last night or early this morning." The deputy paused as the dogs were circling, their noses to the ground. "Found his trail leaving the river and crossing the field. The hounds say he was here."

"Well, of course, he was here," Pa said. "He drove Mrs. Ward here yesterday and stayed all day."

The deputy paused. "Yeah, we know that, but down on the river? We picked up his trail up near town on the bank. We figure he lashed some logs together there and floated down this far. And down there alongside your field is where he came out and run up here to the house. Now where're you hiding him. Might as well tell for the dogs will rout him out quick enough. And you'll be jailed for helping him escape."

Betsy didn't give Pa time to answer. She yelled out, "He ain't here!" That shut everyone up. "He didn't just come off the river. That was yesterday. He was with us down on the river. We went fishing from the bank."

"Yes, they did," Pa said.

"We were on both sides of the river yesterday fishing," I

shouted at the same time that Pa was saying, "You'll find his tracks all over the farm. He and the twins were outside here all day while the ladies were quilting."

I guess we convinced the deputy, for he quieted down the dogs and said sort of apologetically, "Well, I guess we'll have to go on down the bank some more to find where he left the river."

"Rudy drove the Ward's buggy across the ford from their place to come here," I said, for once getting in ahead of Betsy.

"She told him to," Betsy said, "even though the water was high." I could never get in the last word with her. "So his tracks will be there, too."

"Well, we'll just have to go back and keep following the river," the sheriff said. "The hounds will catch his scent, and we will see his boot tracks in this damp ground. He'll be easy to find."

The men turned their dogs back toward the river. 'Course, me, Betsy, and Pa all tagged along behind them. We wouldn't miss this excitement, though we were really scared for Rudy.

And sure enough, when we got to where the trail fords the river up to the Pendletons' place, the hounds picked up the scent. They started howling again and straining on their leashes anxious to run.

"He got off the logs here," the deputy said. He looked up the road and pointed to the Pendletons' house. "He must have gone there."

Betsy couldn't be still any longer. "Rudy drove Mrs. Pendleton in the Ward's buggy to our house yesterday and crossed here. Mrs. Pendleton even told him to get down to make sure the water was safe to cross."

"Yeah," I said. "we were with them. Rudy tramped all over here seeing how high the water was."

The men didn't act like they believed us. They hung onto the dogs' leashes as they splashed across the river and followed the muddy trail up to the Pendletons' back porch. Me, Betsy, and Pa jumped across the river on some rocks.

All that commotion brought both of the Pendletons out their back door.

"Runaway slave," the deputy said. "The Ward houseboy, Rudy. His trail leads here."

"Of course his trail is here," Mrs. Pendleton said. "He was here yesterday. His tracks will be all around here."

The dogs, still dripping water from the river, tried to get into the kitchen.

"But inside the house?" the deputy asked.

"We all went inside to eat cookies," Betsy yelled above the hounds.

"That's right," Mrs. Pendleton said. "I gave the young'uns some cookies." She looked at the table behind her and picked up the platter with just a couple of cookies left. "Here are a few left. Would you like one?"

One of the dogs got almost past the doorway where Mrs. Pendleton was blocking it.

"Get those dirty dogs out of my kitchen," she said sort of mad like, "unless you want to mop the whole place. Yes, Rudy was here, but he was here yesterday with the twins to take me to the quilting party."

In the confusion of dogs baying and people trying to be heard, me and Betsy kept saying that was the way it was. Pa did too. Mrs. Pendleton yelled to keep the dogs out of their house. Mr. Pendleton shouted for everyone to calm down. Finally the men pulled the dogs back onto the porch stoop. "Sorry to bother you, ma'am," the deputy said polite-like. "The slave must have gone on farther down the river, or we missed his trail somewhere." He pulled the dogs around and took them back down to the river.

Betsy nudged me and pointed to the bedroom just off the kitchen. The door was open again. The quilt on the bed was one Ma called a Double Wedding Ring. It wasn't nothing like the colorful pattern of the one we saw her spread on the bed the day before.

"He said he wouldn't be sold," Betsy said whispered.

I nodded.

We breathed easier. It looked like Rudy was safe, and we had almost figured it out how he did it.

For a few days the hunt for Rudy continued. Me and Betsy was with Pa in town when the deputy told what he thought happened. They didn't find Rudy's scent on the river anywhere farther down the river after the Pendletons' crossing. The official report was that he floated on logs down the river into the next county. Then he hightailed it to Kansas, a free state where someone on the underground railroad helped him to Canada where the United States slave law couldn't touch him.

But me and Betsy knew what really happened. All we couldn't figure out was that underground railroad bit. We knew there was lots of caves in our area, but there couldn't be enough strung together to build a railroad all the way to Canada. Why that had to be over a thousand miles!

Betsy didn't said a word while the deputy was explaining this to us, but just as we were leaving his office, she asked what I was dying to know but didn't want to show how dumb I was to ask, "What is the underground railroad?"

"Yeah," I said really showing my stupidity, "there can't be a railroad underground all the way to Canada."

Both Pa and the deputy laughed. Then the deputy sort of bent over to talk to Betsy as if she was a baby or some dumb kid instead of the only one, except me, who figured out what really happened.

"Well, honey, it isn't really a railroad nor is it really under-ground." He stopped then as if trying to figure out how to tell this dumb kid.

"You see, some people break the law that says that everyone must turn in runaway slaves if they see them, even in states where slavery is illegal. They get arrested if they help in any way. But some people break that law and hide runaway slaves in cellars or other places and at night help them to another house along the route to Canada. We are close to Kansas where there are people who hide slaves and help them on their way. In fact, there are whole routes from the south going north that do that quite regularly. That is the Underground Railroad."

"Oh," Betsy said, sneaking a look at me. She'd figured it out like I had.

"So you think Rudy got onto someone that helped him escape?" I asked. I wasn't going to let Betsy get in all the questions.

"Yes, that's what we think?"

"Do you have any idea who that might be in Rudy's case?" Pa asked this. We wanted to but didn't dare ask.

"No, we don't. It's probably someone miles away from here in the next county. There's been some activity there, but it is out of our jurisdiction."

Betsy squeezed my hand as we followed Pa back to our wagon to go home. I looked at her and nodded.

We know everything now. Like that modern telegraph that sends messages over wire, we do it with our eyes. We know what the other is thinking. Maybe because we are twins. Without talking it over, we both know the quilt on Mrs. Pendleton's bed was a signal to Rudy. It is some sort of special pattern that the slaves know about that means their house is a station on the underground railroad.

We also know why Mrs. Pendleton insisted on Rudy coming into her kitchen for cookies. And why she had us cross the dangerous ford and why she had Rudy get down from the buggy and walk all over the bank. All that was to leave his tracks and his scent for the blood hounds. He made an honest trail to mask the one he would make later that night as he escaped to her house. We also know that Rudy was in their house when the deputies and the hounds were there. The hounds' dirty feet weren't the only reason Mrs. Pendleton wouldn't let them inside. And we know why Mr. Pendleton has so much business in Kansas and that he made the trip across the border later that same night. But no one else knows. We won't tell. Ever.

The End

– Ellen Gray Massey

born at Nevada, Missouri, has lived in Laclede County, Missouri, since 1946 and taught for forty-two years in elementary and high schools, and as adjunct faculty for Drury University's Graduate Education Program. She has taught Road Scholar (formerly Elderhostel) classes for the YMCA of the Ozarks at, and for Ozark Adventures in Branson. A prolific speaker and writer, she promotes the Ozarks tirelessly. Since 1990 she has given over 400 talks about the Ozarks and about writing. She was teacher/advisor from 1973-1983 of *Bittersweet, the Ozark Quarterly*, published by her students at Lebanon High School and has done other editorial work professionally and for friends.

Ellen has published numerous articles, short stories, essays, a musical play, as well as 17 novels and 12 non-fiction books. In 1995 she was inducted into the first Writers Hall of Fame of America. She has received 25 awards from the Missouri Writers Guild and three times finalist in Western Writers of America's Golden Spur Awards.

Her recent non-fiction books are *Footprints in the Ozarks: a Memoir* and *Our Robin Is Read: Voices from The Wayside* by

Goldminds Publishing. Recent novels are *Brothers, Blue and Gray and Her Enemies, Blue and Gray* by Gold-minds Publishing, *Skeleton in the Cistern* in Kindle, and *Papa's Gold* by Pen-L Publishing.

Her website is www.ellengraymassey.com

Desert Rose – Bounty Hunter

by Kathi Sprayberry

A flat-brimmed hat shaded her startling blue eyes and creamy complexion. Coal black, curly hair bounced and flipped against her back, drawing sweat from her dust-stained white shirt. A split skirt in muddy brown encased slender legs that gripped the flanks of the horse upon which she rode. Rose O'Cannon, survivor of one of the infamous coffin ships leaving Ireland during the Great Potato Famine, stared hard at the unrelenting desert landscape surrounding Tombstone, Arizona Territory. Here she began her quest three years past and here she would end an unrelenting search when she captured the men responsible for killing the last of her family.

"Tis nothing but sorrow for the O'Cannon's since those men did their vile work," Rose murmured. "I be not the last, but the name dies with me daughter. Oh, the shame of it! What the English and the famine failed to accomplish, those murdering scum did."

Sorrow settled around Rose like a heavy blanket. Most of her four and twenty years had been spent grieving family taken from her by the English invaders in her homeland or other circumstances. Since losing her aunt, uncle, and cousins, Rose's life consisted of travel from town to town in the untamed West. She sought miscreants for the rewards offered in return for their capture. Because of her diminutive stature and gender, the criminals she tracked down always resisted. Her fast draw and dead-on aim earned her the moniker Desert Rose, bounty hunter.

"This one's for free, Bailintin." Rose leaned forward to pat her horse's neck; the gelding's name came from the ancient Irish language, Gaelic, and meant Valiant. "This one is for Uncle Liam, Aunt Kathleen, and me cousins."

A bit of the Irish speech crept into her voice as yearning took her heart. Rose carried a taint upon her soul, a taint that killed her parents and five brothers during the long journey from Ireland to New York City. She firmly believed the same taint brought about the famine in her homeland. Three centuries earlier, the Spanish Armada washed ashore near her family's home. The Spaniards pillaged the land and ravished many a young woman. Now, in every generation of O'Cannon's, one female carried the looks of those marauders and brought bad luck upon those close to her.

"We break the curse forever today." Rose straightened and stared at the town on the horizon. "Tombstone's where those men lit and Tombstone's where I shall bring them in – alive."

Never far from her memories, the past took hold of Rose. Twelve at the time she watched her parents and brothers buried at sea, she overcame the sorrow before her fourteenth birthday by helping her aunt, uncle, and cousins build their desert ranch between Tombstone and Charleston. Then came the moonless night on the eve of her twenty-first birthday when three bandits crept through her bedroom window; men who never bothered covering their faces. They had their way with her and one knifed Rose's neck when she wailed out her terror. Unconsciousness took her only seconds into a heated gun battle with bullets whistling all around and she woke to yet again having lost those she loved.

"They'll pay." Rose pushed the horrific memories into the far reaches of her mind, to better concentrate on the task at hand. "No one will stop me."

Since taking up the bounty hunter profession, Rose brought in her quarries without a breath of life in their bodies, but these men were different. Miners and bandits they were; they took up with a group of men wreaking havoc all over the area – the cowboys.

Rose knew the English enforcing the law in Tombstone were as corrupt as those they took every opportunity to harass or jail. John Behan vowed to protect Uncle Liam's ranch and family. Behan claimed kinship, as one Irishman to another. Yet, when bandits he called bosom buddies entered the adobe house in 1879, the man made himself scarce. Behan showed his true colors to Rose after she recovered from what were supposed to be mortal injuries.

"No one will stop me from seeing those men swing." Rose fingered the scar along her neck, her fingers stopping when the ridged skin met the high collar of her blouse. "No matter if I need to send a wire to the marshal service in Washington DC, I'll make sure Charles Boyden, Mick Angelo, and Tom Higgins pay the price for my pain."

She let her gaze move north and west, in the direction of the convent where she sought refuge after discovering those men did more than violate her body; one left behind a wee bairn. The daughter Rose bore, Caitlyn, spookily resembled her mother in looks and temperament. Thanks to the nuns at Mission San Xavier del Bac, the child had a home where Rose visited whenever she was close. The nuns treated the child with loving care and swore never to reveal the act which brought her into this world.

"Keep me babe safe, Lord," Rose uttered the words to a prayer she said daily. "Protect her from the ugliness in this harsh world."

A nudge of her heels prodded the horse into a gentle trot. Rose swayed in the saddle, her hand hovering near a shotgun she kept in its boot near her left leg. Tombstone loomed closer and closer, as did the sense of evil surrounding the area. As fey as her ancestors, Rose ignored warnings to turn and run for her sanity.

Premonitions of trouble would never keep her from completing
this quest. She then planned to make her way east, back to New
York City and onto a boat to return to Mother Ireland, but only
after she collected her daughter and purchased a wedding band.
No one would ever know Caitlyn had no father nor had her
mother wed the monster responsible for her sorrow.

Rose allowed herself a moment of weakness as a tear rolled
alongside her nose. She longed for the barely remembered
breezes coming off the Irish Sea. Yearning seared her damaged
soul for the gentle green hills of the land and the soothing brogue
of her kind. Americans spoke in harsh voices and too many were
of the dreaded English ancestry, especially those she must deal
with this day.

"Or week," she whispered, her words carrying on the constant
wind laden with gritty sand driven from the ground by dust
devils. "However long it takes. John Behan nor any of the Earps
will stop me."

Small ranches, much like her Uncle Liam's, appeared on
either side of her. Rose gave them a cursory glance, no more. The
activities of those ranchers bothered her not, so long as none of
the men herding cattle attempted to stop her. Bailintin's gait
picked up and Rose leaned forward as the raucous town of Tombstone came into view. Rarely did the town go entirely quiet, but it
had changed so much since the last time she saw its streets. Far
more people wandered along boardwalks in front of stores and
she gaped like a child let loose in a circus. She closed her mouth
and began a methodical search for a place to lay her head. Tonight, after the families she saw everywhere retired to their
homes, she would begin her search in the saloons.

A jail near Schieffelin Hall drew Rose's attention and she
pulled on the reins until Bailintin stopped. A sight she never
thought to see amazed the young woman. Two of the Englishmen
she hated stood together at the top of the steps. John Behan
lounged against a wall beside a rough wooden door while Wyatt

and Morgan Earp examined the street beside and around Rose. She stared at them until Morgan sashayed down the steps and stood beneath her gaze.

"May I help you, ma'am." A quizzical expression crossed Morgan's face. "Forgive me for being forward but do I know you?"

A silver badge proclaiming his status as a city policeman decorated his left chest, in a perfect position for one of the cowboys to use the tin star as a target. Rose permitted herself a rare smile at having the means to dispatch one of the men who failed her three years back at her disposal.

"Do ye know me?" she asked, the Irish lilt becoming more pronounced with each word. "Did ye forget what happened in September of 1879, Morgan?"

"My brothers and I arrived the first of December that year," he replied. "But I still believe we've met at some time."

Morgan squinted and took in her face in an examination that lasted long enough for Wyatt to join them. The older Earp, a man with legends already attached to his name from his time in Dodge City, pinned Rose in her saddle with a glare that would have murdered a lesser person.

"Rose O'Cannon," Wyatt said with barely restrained fury. "I've heard you took up bounty hunting." His voice took on a sarcastic tone. "Desert Rose, very original."

"Aye, I did. The name fits since the desert failed to sear this rose." Rose dismounted in one smooth move and tied off Bailintin to the hitching rail in front of the jail. "Isn't John Behan about to make this unholy trio more than I can stand? Two English and an English bootlicker are far too much for my delicate sensibilities. Don't you agree?" She easily fell into the Irish way of making observations into questions. "Shall I leave you to your useless musings and get about me business?"

She pushed past the men and sauntered into the jail, removing her hat as she entered. Using the hat to smack dust from her split skirt, Rose examined the board beside the door, searching for bounties on the men she sought. To her disappointment, none existed.

"You won't find what you seek there," a gravelly voice said. "Leave Tombstone, Desert Rose. Your fast draw and even faster trigger finger will only cause more headaches; headaches I don't need. I have yet to put a woman into my jail but I will if you remain in Tombstone."

Rose turned and smiled, a smile full of the promise of violence. "My, my. Can ye explain why you leave your brothers to stand with John Behan while you rest your legs in here, Virgil Earp?" He also wore a badge; the badge naming him town marshal. "Did the town council lose control of their senses, Virgil Earp? Truly, I don't understand this at all, at all. Two Earps, both English, given leave to make so many lives miserable? Tis truly a quandary I want no part of."

"Leave Tombstone, Rose," Virgil repeated. "I won't have my town shot up whilst you search for the men you claim killed your family."

"And have they proved to ye, Marshal Virgil Earp, they were never near me uncle's piddllin' ranch that night?" Rose thrust out her chin in a belligerent manner. "Can ye find none who say otherwise? Can none of their friends give them up to ye for the reward I left to be posted?"

"You took long enough to report the crime," he retorted. "I have no way of knowing if the witnesses spoke the truth when I questioned them more than three months after the fact."

"Nor did ye try very hard," she shot back. "What's one or a dozen less Irish in this world to an Englishman?"

Virgil Earp rose from the chair upon which he sat and crossed the room until he stared down at Rose.

"Behan claimed those men played poker with him from approximately six in the evening until well past dawn the day after the attack on your family," Virgil announced. "We never

pursued charges against them, as Behan had other witnesses."
His mouth twisted into a grimace. "Men known as the cowboys."

"And, of course, ye believe everything spouting from that
English bootlicker's lips, do ye?" Rose silently cursed her short
stature that put her at an extreme disadvantage with this tower-
ing hulk of disapproval. "I swore it then and I will do the same
now. Charles Boyden, Mick Angelo, and Tom Higgins attacked
Uncle Liam's ranch. Those bandits tried to slit me throat and left
me for dead while shooting everyone else in the house." She
jerked her head to one side and trailed a finger across the still
vivid scar. "Isn't that enough proof for ye, Marshal Virgil Earp?
Do ye doubt me word when I tell you they stopped at the ranch
earlier in the day but left angry when Uncle Liam and Aunt Kathleen refused to pay them tribute?"

The door creaked open. Behan, Morgan, and Wyatt moved
behind Virgil. The lawmen glowered their disapproval at her
words. Even Wyatt, though he wore no badge, stood firm against
her. August heat caused sweat to pour down her face, stinging
her already tender eyes.

"Believe me or not!" Rose exclaimed. "I thought to wait until
nightfall to begin me search but your lack of concern for this
town's women convinces me otherwise. I shall bring those men
to you before sunset – alive. Then I shall swear out a complaint
of murder against them." Unbidden tears clouded her vision.
"They will never do that again."

Angered beyond belief, Rose made to push through the wall of
men. None but Morgan moved aside. She held her head high and
met incredulous but puzzled looks from the other three.

"Let Rose leave," Morgan said in a quiet but commanding
voice. "She'll do as she said. We have no worries about her
starting a gunfight."

Behan, Wyatt, and Virgil stepped aside. Rose stormed out of
the jail and slammed the door. She slapped the hat atop her un-
ruly hair and paused until her emotions settled.

"By all that's holy, what do you think you're doing?" Wyatt's explosive bellow penetrated the jail's wooden walls. "Desert Rose has never brought in a bounty alive."

"She will this time," Morgan insisted. "Or do I have to remind you about another young woman and the way she reacted to men." His voice grew sharper. "I can't believe you don't remember that incident in Dodge City, Wyatt. You told me it haunts you."

No!" Wyatt gasped. "Are you saying—"

"I am," Morgan responded in a firm tone. "And that's as far as I'll take this discussion. Rose will bring in the men she saw that night, have no doubts of that."

The sound of boots stomping toward the door prodded Rose into action. She stopped when Behan yelled.

"I already told you those men played poker with me that night! What will it take for you to believe me?"

"Witnesses other than cowboys," Virgil said. "And a woman not so certain of what she saw, heard, and experienced. I had my doubts then and now, those doubts grow stronger, Behan. It's well-known you'll do anything for certain people in this town."

With a smile of satisfaction at the English bootlicker's turn of fortunes, Rose walked down the steps and yanked her shotgun from its boot. She strode along Fremont Street's boardwalk, stopping to peer through batwings on the many saloons. Men stared at her with mouths gaping while women shooed their children to dubious safety within several stores. At Sixth Street, she turned and kept an eye on the Red Light District as she made her way to Allen.

"So many saloons," Rose commented as she sauntered along the boardwalk. "No wonder Virgil says he has headaches. When do any of these men have time to work?"

It was on Allen Street, midway between Fifth and Fourth Streets, where Rose heard a familiar voice. She pushed open the batwings on Campbell & Hatches Saloon and stood in the door-way.

"Wimmen ain't allowed without a man," the barkeep said in a bored tone. "Not unless you're a whore. Iffen you are, git into something more revealing and put your arse to work."

Rose ignored his profane comment and stared at a table in the far corner. Three men clad in the dusty gray pants and shirts preferred by miners stared at her. She jacked a round into the shotgun and took aim.

"This scattergun makes my finger itch," Rose spoke her trademark statement in an almost bored tone. "Get your carcasses up."

"Do you really think a bitty thing like you can take us alive?" Charles Boyden demanded. "We'll teach you a few manners, missy. Barkeep." He turned toward the bar. "Send a boy for Marshal Earp. He'll take care of this hoyden."

"My name is Desert Rose," Rose said.

Dead silence greeted her announcement. Mick Angelo and Tom Higgins edged away from Charles and raised their hands into the air. Charles gulped and stared at her.

"Desert Rose?" Charles squeaked. "Why are you after us? There ain't no bounty on our names."

"Only because an English bootlicker gave you an alibi," Rose told him in even tones. "But I know what you did on September 4, 1879 at Liam O'Cannon's ranch Your only mistake was in not making sure I died from the knife ye used to slit me throat, Charles Boyden."

Ach, but her shame was now out for all to know. Not only had these men destroyed her purity but the one who fathered her child was also of English ancestry. Rose vowed then and there to keep that information from her wee bairn. Caitlyn would never live with that shame.

"Tis a lie," Charles claimed. "We played poker with Sheriff John Behan that night."

"Shut your mouth," Mick Angelo cried. "She's holding a scattergun on us."

"Ach, and me finger just itches to cut ye down for what ye did,"

Rose answered calmly. "The English have done worse in the homeland but I'm thinking a few less English by me hand won't make no never mind. Don't ye agree?"

The men's faces leached white, so white it appeared they might faint. The barkeep edged away from the center of the room and ducked through a rear door.

"Move," Rose ordered. "In front of me, and none of you even think about trying to grab me gun. It has a hair trigger." She smiled; this one indifferent. "I promised Marshal Earp to deliver ye alive. It wouldn't do to go back on me word, would it?"

The sun had moved to halfway between noon and sunset when Rose marched the three men responsible for her worst misery and greatest joy along Allen Street. At Fourth Street, she ordered them to turn toward Fremont and once more until they stopped in front of the jail.

"Virgil Earp," Rose called in a loud, clear voice. "I've done as I promised. No one died this day. I'll still swear out that complaint."

Wyatt, Morgan, and Virgil spilled out of the jail with their guns drawn. Their mouths dropped open at the sight of three grown men quivering in front of Rose. She lowered the shotgun.

"Do ye need me statement now or may I come back on the morrow?" Rose asked.

"Tomorrow will be fine," Virgil sputtered. "Where will you stay?"

"The Palace Hotel." Rose stared at him hard. "Do ye believe me now?"

Behan still had not come out of the jail, if he was still in there. Rose tilted her head and examined the surprise etched into the Earp's faces.

"We believe you, Rose," Morgan managed to say. "Come back tomorrow about ten. We'll take your statement and notify the judge he's needed up here."

Tired both in body and heart, Rose trudged away, one hand holding onto Bailintin's reins. The gelding would never again carry her from town to town in an effort to stop murderers from tearing apart families. She felt nothing more than relief at the thought of having a life free of violence.

"Tis truly a great day, Bailintin," Rose said as she spotted the Palace Hotel. "Ye will have a life of luxury, all the hay and corn you can handle and paddocks of green grass to frolic in. Me? I shall finally have a home."

Ireland's beckoning call waned. She looked around for a reason to abandon her quest to return to her homeland. Sure, and it was a beautiful place to live, but the English invaders made life near impossible for the Irish. Her eyes lit upon Morgan Earp a few feet away. He stared at her with bottomless eyes.

"Why do ye trail after me?" Rose demanded. "Have I perhaps broken some law I don't know of?"

"No." Morgan approached her carefully, almost as if he expected her to bolt. "I have to know something. You call us English. What meaning does that have?"

"You be English, don't ye?" She asked.

This man, this enemy, seemed to care about her, but that was wrong. All the English cared about was destroying the Irish. Sure, and did they not do that so much in the homeland?

"My family originally came from England," Morgan conceded. "But we're Americans now, as are you."

"Nay." She shook her head. "I shall always be Irish. Tis part of my soul, the motherland with her gentle rains and loving people."

"And you'll always hate anyone from England?" he asked.

"Mayhaps." Rose nodded. "Are not the English responsible for Irish misery? Do they not have a boot on our necks? Did they not send families away from the motherland in ships destined to kill nearly half those aboard? Do not the English decide we must speak their blasted language instead of our own? Do they not call us savages while they ravage our women and murder our men?"

"I have no idea of conditions in Ireland," Morgan said. "But I see a beautiful woman with pain in her past, searching for a way to ease that pain. Running away to a place where she'll experience more of that pain seems wrong to me."

"Aye, ye may be right." Rose walked the last few steps to the hotel. "I'll think on it, Englishman. But don't think I'll stay around here, either."

"I didn't expect that," Morgan replied. "I'll see you tomorrow."

He tipped his hat in a gesture of respect and walked off. Rose stared at his back for a long time as his words penetrated the numbness in her brain. All the plans she had made to return to Ireland now seemed wrong, all wrong.

"Tis a difficult decision," she said. "But one I'll have to make before I bring me Caitlyn to this place, even if it's only for a few hours."

Inside the hotel, she paid a lad to send a telegram to the mission for her. Rose spent an hour in a hot tub and then had a good meal before seeking out a dressmaker. Her new persona, that of loving mother, required her to give up her bounty hunting attire. Her last errand saddened Rose but keeping Bailintin was out of the question. The liveryman paid her an excellent price for such a well cared for gelding and promised green paddocks if the right man discovered the animal. By the time she settled in her bed for the night, the difficult decision resolved itself. Ireland was a wonderful dream but the reality was the country still had far too many problems for her to raise a child there without constant worry.

Precisely at ten the next morning, Rose marched into the jail and gave her statement of the events three years ago. She left out the part about the men assaulting her and how her cries caused the gun battle that killed her aunt, uncle, and cousins. Morgan finished writing out her complaint and had her sign the paper.

"Judge'll be up here in ten days," Morgan said. "He said the trial would probably only last a day or two. Will you stay?"

"Aye." Rose nodded. "I have nothing else to do except make arrangements for me future. May I leave? I have much to do."

"In a minute." He smiled. "Are you still returning to Ireland?"

"Mayhaps, but I think not," Rose said with great reluctance. "I have an idea about where'll I'll settle but no one else will know." She lowered her voice to where it was near impossible to hear. "No one but one other."

She walked out of the jail. Forever loomed on the horizon and she was eager to find out what fate had in mind for her.

Two weeks later, Rose watched as the men who stole her innocence and murdered eight people swung from the gallows. She felt no pity when they begged for their lives; just as they showed no pity for her family on that bloody night. After the last one finished kicking, she walked away with a far lighter heart.

"Let the stage be on time," she whispered.

The stagecoach station appeared deserted. Rose stood in front of the building and watched for a dust cloud from the northwest. Forty minutes later, her vigil was rewarded. Eagerness rose within her. One hand on the hitching post, she strained to see the coach. Soon, it barreled toward her. As soon as the driver braked, she raced for the door as it opened.

A tiny replica of herself jumped down without assistance and dashed to Rose. She grabbed her daughter and held her tight. So grand was their reunion, Rose ignored the woman clad in black from head to toe who came off the stage after Caitlyn. Sister Brighid always stayed within steps of the child, but now, after almost three years, that duty was now Rose's.

"Ach, me Caitlyn," Rose cried. "We'll never be apart again."

Their reunion brought gentle healing to the horrific wounds Rose suffered so long ago. She and the child cried out tearful remembrances of the few times they spent together. Rose held her daughter high in the air, studying all the changes since they last had a few hours to visit. Some of the baby fat had vanished and Caitlyn showed signs of great beauty later. The wee bairn stared back at her mother with a look of awe.

"I love you, Mama!" Caitlyn declared.

"Ach, and don't I love you as much?" Rose returned and held her daughter tight in another hug.

The sound of measured footsteps from behind failed to upset Rose. So long as she held Caitlyn, Rose felt safe. The warm bundle of love rained kisses all over her face and neck. So far as Rose was concerned, all was right in the world – finally.

"So that's who you protected," Morgan said from behind Rose.

Frightened out of her mind, Rose pulled the child closer to her chest. Caitlyn wiggled around and peered at the lawman. Slowly, ever so slowly, Rose faced the man capable of destroying her new-found happiness.

"If I deny your suspicions?" Rose asked.

"The child is about two," he said in a bland tone. "I may not have a child of my own, but I know how fiercely mothers protect their young. Why did you not tell us about this, Rose?"

"Mama, what's he talking about?" Caitlyn piped in her childish voice.

"Nothing, me babe," Rose answered. "Nothing at all." She glared at Morgan. "Aye, Morgan, mothers will do whatever's necessary to protect their young."

"Then you're off to Ireland?" he asked.

"Nay," she said with a shake of her head. "But far from here. The desert has begun to wilt this rose. I'm thinking me and me bairn will settle near San Francisco."

"I'll warn the law up there," Morgan said with a smile. "But, somehow, I don't think we'll hear of the bounty hunter, Desert Rose, again."

"Aye," Rose said. "Desert Rose has taken her last bounty."

She turned away from Morgan and greeted Sister Brighid. An exchange of a bank draft for the good sisters at the mission made the difficult parting easier for Rose but not the nun nor the child. Sister Brighid boarded the stagecoach and Rose followed after the stage driver loaded the few trunks containing her belongings. Within the hour, when the stage returned to Tucson, Rose sat at the window with her daughter at her side. The ache Rose had carried for so long began to subside.

The End

– Kathi Sprayberry

is the author of several "Best of" winning Tales. Her teen novel, *Softly Say Goodbye,* was published by Solstice in 2013.

Kathi's stories have appeared in many magazines for teens, and in four anthologies *Passionate Hearts Anthology* (2010), *Mystery Times Ten* (2011), *The Best of Frontier Tales, Vol. I* (2012), and *Mystery Times Nine* (2012).

Her interest in telling her stories goes back to her high school years. While she spends many days researching areas of interest,  she also loves photography and often uses it as a way to integrate scenery into her work. She lives in Northwest Georgia with her husband and youngest son. She's on Twitter: @kcsowriter.

Payback at Murderer's Bar

by John Putnam

Sunshine suddenly flooded through the open door of the cabin. I picked up the crutch my eldest, Enos, had fashioned from an alder branch and limped outside. Thick, dark clouds still roiled above the river as far as I could see, but off to the west a small gap between heaven and earth had given the setting sun a last brief opportunity to remind us of the glory of its existence.

It was a welcome sign. Rain had fallen in a steady downpour since yesterday morning, starting just after we'd finally finished work on the flume. All summer long nearly four hundred men, most new to California, had toiled together to this one end. We'd even hauled a horse-powered sawmill up from Sacramento to turn the trees of the canyon into lumber. When it looked like we weren't going to finish on time we'd toted piles of canvas in by mule back and painstakingly stitched it across a wooden frame twelve feet wide by three feet high that stretched more than a mile downstream.

Using more heavy timber reinforced with rock, we'd built a wing dam a hundred yards upstream that crossed to the gravel of Murderer's Bar where it hooked up with the flume. The whole thing was carefully contrived to direct the water down the canvas-covered chute so that we could mine the riverbed. Men had already pulled most of the gold from the bars and gullies above the waterline but an unimaginable bounty still lay at the bottom of the stream. During a short break from the rain this morning two men had dug out over nine pounds of gold before breakfast. Everyone was eager to get started.

The river had swollen quickly during the storm and brought a new power to the flow that could be seen clearly in the fury of the water tumbling over the falls above Murderer's Bar. The rain had caused a lot of consternation here and men were busy piling more rock near the dam just to be sure it held. Still, we could use a few days of sun to dry the stream's bed. Miners who'd been in California a while said September was way too early for a storm this strong and we could expect many more days as hot as any we'd seen all summer. They figured the sun would be back in all its might by morning.

For miles above the falls more men had joined together with the same purpose as we had, and more dams and flumes were now being built far upstream, even into the high mountains. The Middle Fork of the American River had proven to be as rich a mining site as Mormon Island or Hangtown, and thanks to our hard work a vast fortune now sat exposed in the belly of the river, leaving us awaiting only a favorable change in the weather to realize the goals of our long suffering summer of toil. Each man here fully expected a payback many times his expenditures in both hard cash and hot sweat.

Just as I turned to go back inside I saw Rawley, my youngest, coming up the hill wearing his black India rubber coat, a rain sopped felt hat, and britches and boots caked with mud. With his head down, never once looking up, hands jammed in his pockets, he kicked away a rock in his path and cursed. The boy was a handful, almost grown and headstrong. Sarah said he needed extra love. Maybe I didn't have enough to spare.

"Evening, son. Supper's almost ready. Where's your brother?" I called out.

He looked up at me with a sneer. "Why should I care where Mister Enos Oates is?" he carped as he bulled past me and into the cabin.

Just then, with the sun still shining low on the horizon, the rain broke again, coming down hard and sudden. I ducked inside behind Rawley, pulling the door closed after me. He stood by his bunk, holding his rifle, checking to see if it was loaded.

"What are you doing?" I demanded.

"Going hunting," he growled, his words dripping with his rage.

"No you're not," I countered. "It's raining like the dickens again. You can't hunt an animal in a storm like this."

"Depends on the animal," he said, much too coldly.

"Put that gun down, right now." I barked, my old anger starting to rise. "What happened between you and Enos?"

Rawley pulled the gun to his shoulder and sighted along the barrel. "What happened between me and my big brother, you ask?" He spat my words back, mocking me after all I'd done for him, after all his brother had done for him. "What always happens between me and your oldest son, your favorite son?" he continued. "'You're not good enough to do this, Rawley. You're not smart enough to figure that out, little brother. Just shut up and do as I tell you, jackass.'" His tone had grown louder and more sullen as he raged. He pulled the gun down and waved a hand over his head. "Well I've had it up to here. Now I'm going to end it once and for all. Get out of my way."

"So you're going to shoot your own brother." I roared back. "Is that the answer? He'll be dead and you'll hang. What'll that get anybody? How will your mother feel when she hears? It'll kill her and you know it. Is that what you want?"

He spun away from me. "What am I supposed to do? I can't take it anymore." I heard the same whine in his voice I'd heard for years. His anger was spent now. He was done. I'd won again, but what would happen if one day I wasn't here to stop him?

"Put the rifle down, Rawley," I said softly. When he didn't answer right off I hobbled over and took it from his hand. He didn't resist. I knew he wouldn't.

He collapsed on his bunk, his face to the wall, sulking like he always did after one of his set-tos with Enos. Sarah understood him. She could reason with him, calm him down, but he didn't listen to me. As much as I loved him I reckon it wasn't enough. It was times like this that I wished I'd left him in Ohio with his mother.

I propped the rifle in the corner, limped over to the fireplace and rested my crutch against the chimney, built only from sticks and mud sitting on top of a flat stone firebox it still drew the smoke out well enough. The cabin itself was made of rough pine logs with the bark still on and roofed over with sod. It was barely big enough to sleep the three of us, but we had it better than many and I, for one, was grateful for that.

The stew had simmered all afternoon but the beef we'd gotten yesterday had been stringy and tough, the cow all skin and bones. I took a taste. Even the hours of boiling hadn't helped much. Still it was all we had. It would have to do. Fortunately the flour I'd bought had been good quality and we would have enough bread for a while. I gave the pot a quick stir just as the door burst open and Enos strode in.

He shook the rain from his hat then pulled off the rubber coat as he stomped his boots, knocking mud onto the dirt floor. Six years older than Rawley, he'd grown into a fine man, tall and well built with keen eyes that pierced straight to the heart. A natural leader, men listened to him and did what he said. He'd taken control of one part of the work we'd done on the dam, overseeing the crew who had driven the pilings into the streambed then lined them with timbers and finally loaded rock on the waterfall side.

"Evening, Pa," he said as he pulled up a stool opposite me.

"What happened with you and Rawley this time?" I asked without hesitation. Nothing hurt me worse than when my sons fought.

"You know how he is. He won't listen to what you tell him to do. He's always got another idea, a different way of doing things. He just can't put his back into something and get it done. He kept after me till I had to slap him around some to shut him up."

"You hit him first?" I asked with some fire in my tone. To me words would never hurt a man but the one who threw the first blow was always in the wrong.

"Well, after he shoved me, Pa. I couldn't have that."

"That's a lie!" Rawley yelled from his bed. "You just hauled off and punched me. And it's you who don't listen. You've got to put more rock on the backside of the dam where the flume is. That's the weak point. That's where it'll bust if too much water comes down river. Then the flume will float off like a giant canoe."

I looked deep into Enos' eyes. "Is what he says true?" I ask.

"I said he pushed me, Pa and he did."

'Liar! See, Enos won't listen to me about the dam!" Rawley yelled.

"Quiet, both of you. I'll have no more of this." I bellowed. "What about the dam busting at the flume like Rawley said, can that happen?"

"Pa, anything can happen. You know that. But Rawley's got too many wild ideas, always reading, wanting to go that fancy school. He already thinks he's an engineer. Nobody can tell if that dam will break or where. The men are tired. They worked hard all day in the storm. They need a break. The sun'll be out tomorrow anyway."

"What if you're wrong, big brother?" Rawley hissed the words in that way he had of acting too big for his own britches and I could see Enos' face darken. It's no wonder he slapped the boy around some. Rawley could be like one of those little dogs that never stop nipping at your heels as you walk down the street, a real pain in the rump.

From somewhere outside the harsh squawks of a blue jay drowned out the sweet warble of the wrens. Bright light streaked through chinks in the log walls so I sat up, stretched my arms wide and yawned, then saw Enos on a stool pulling up his boots.

"How's your ankle today, Pa?" he asked.

I bent my knee and felt my leg. "Better I think, the swelling's down some," I said.

He stood. "The rain's gone. It's a fine day and we've got gold to mine. Are you able to work?" he said as he walked across the room.

"Expect I can do something anyway. Aren't you having breakfast?" I grabbed my crutch and pushed myself from my cot just as Enos jerked open the door.

"There's too much to do, Pa. I'll be back at noon."

I noticed Rawley's empty bunk. "Where's your brother?" I called after him.

Enos stopped just beyond the opening. "Don't know. He was gone when I woke. See you later," he said and the door slammed shut behind him.

It wasn't like Rawley to be up and about before anyone else. He usually slept as late as he could. But more important, his rifle was gone from the corner where I'd left it yesterday. A terrible fear crept up my spine. Maybe he really had gone hunting, and I'd be the last one to fault him for looking for fresh meat after that stringy beef we ate last night, but try as I might, I couldn't shake a burning dread as malevolent as any thought to ever to intrude upon my mind. Could Rawley be planning to kill Enos like he'd threatened? Could I have failed both my sons so badly?

I rushed to the door as fast as my game leg would allow, flung it open and hobbled out. Sunshine flooded my eyes. I raised my hand to block the glare. The falls above Murderer's Bar had grown into a frothing cataract, but the wing dam had held firm and the turbulent waters of the rain-swollen river cascaded down the flume exactly as planned.

Up and down the canyon men poured from shacks, shanties and tents, shovels in hand, racing for the empty riverbed, thirsting for the rewards that now lay at their feet. But nowhere could I could see any sign of Rawley, from the bend in the river far downstream all the way back up to the dam. Directly below our cabin Enos worked with two men, tossing ore into a rocker, then adding water to wash away the black sand in which the gold hid, leaving the heavier metal imbedded along cleats nailed to the bottom.

The frenzy of the men mining the streambed spread faster than a yawn in a country schoolhouse as one man after another thrust a fist high overhead in triumph at the discovery of a particularly large nugget. And I could feel the fever wax within me. I had to get to Enos, into the riverbed, and with my own bare hands pull out the gold that I'd dreamed of so often through the sweltering heat of the long summer. I had to personally experience the thrill of the ultimate redemption; the well-earned payback for all that was justly due me for the hardship I had endured.

I tucked the crutch tight under my arm and, ignoring the pangs that rippled up my leg each time my sprained foot hit the ground, I scuffled as best I could along the path that zigzagged down the canyon, my lust for wealth fueling an impatience as fierce as any I'd ever known. And then I saw him step from behind a boulder halfway to the dam. He raised the rifle to his shoulder and aimed it directly at Enos.

"Rawley!" I screamed with all the force my aging lungs could muster, but a low bass roar louder than that from a hundred riverboats swallowed whole my pitiful cry. Above Rawley a wall of water higher than a house loomed above the falls, then collapsed into the pond behind the dam, carrying with it a forest of timber from dozens of other wing dams and flumes swept away by an overwhelming onslaught rushing down from the mountains above.

A large wave washed into the dam, smashing apart on the rocks into a thick spray that showered over the miners working below. Men broke and ran for the bank, all except Enos, who headed for the dam, slogging through the thick mud of the river's bottom. Rawley coolly followed him with the rifle and I hurried on toward my youngest son, limping badly but bent on stopping him before it was too late.

Timber, brush, mud and canvas continued to crash over the falls then washed up to the flume where it stuck. There it blocked the opening and reduced the flow of the water down the chute to a trickle. With nowhere else to go the swollen river quickly backed up behind the barrier into which we'd invested so much of our honest sweat.

Enos managed to climb up onto the flume just as water began to pour over the dam. He set himself atop the pile of debris now threatening to destroy all our hard work and pulled out whatever timber he could pry loose from the tangle and tossed it into the cataract below, where the water, already higher than two days ago, continued to rise.

I was almost to Rawley when he suddenly dropped the rifle and pointed. "The flume's busted loose. It's floating," he yelled to anyone within earshot.

I stopped my gimpy hobble and turned to follow where his finger led. The canvas chute, now empty of water, had pulled free of its underpinnings and bobbed like a cork on the surface of the rapidly swelling stream. A slow undulation began that grew wider and more intense as the bloated level of the water reached farther downstream.

"It's going to break free," Rawley screamed and as soon as he spoke I heard timber connections all along the flume snap like twigs, allowing even wider swings in the chute. Then, with an ominous crack, the flume broke loose and slithered away down the flooded canyon like a cottonmouth snake on a millpond. The pile of debris that had blocked the chute, now unfettered at the dam and with Enos still on top, swung inland toward Murderer's Bar and broke apart.

Try as he might, there was no way for Enos to keep his balance. He tumbled headlong into the powerful surge that roared through the now open gap where the flume had once been attached and disappeared beneath the churning murk. I stood there, unable to move, unable to think, unable to believe that my oldest son was gone, but nowhere on the surface of the flood was there any sign of him.

Then a cry arose from many throats together and all around me men pointed to the river, and there, in the middle of the floating debris pile, I could see Enos at last, face down, unmoving, washed downstream by the unstoppable flow of water, but because I stood well below the dam he was coming toward me. Only one thought filled my mind, no matter what, no matter how, I must save my son. I abandoned the zigzag path to the river and headed straight downhill as fast as my aching ankle would tolerate.

After only a few lumbering yards, with my eyes locked on Enos instead of the steep slope I'd dared navigate, my good foot caught on a root and I tumbled down the hill. Unhurt, save the remnants of my useless pride, and more determined than ever to rescue my oldest son, I pushed myself back on my feet. But before I could brave another step strong hands grabbed my arms, a finger thrust past my face and a voice at my side cried, "Look there, it's Rawley."

My eyes followed the thrusting finger to the edge of the river. There they locked on Rawley, stripped to his long johns, boots gone, as he dove headfirst into the foaming scumgullion. All around me voices cheered encouragement as my youngest son stroked his way across the muddy current towards Enos, then, almost as one, they cried a loud warning as a particularly large timber bore down on him as he swam. When Rawley ducked from sight my heart leapt to my throat. An anxious gasp rose from the crowd followed quickly by a breathless hush that to me seemed without end.

Then Rawley's head popped from the stream, in two strong strokes he was at Enos' side and in no time had his older brother's head out of the water. A quiet murmur began, much like the buzz of bees moving steadily closer, but when Rawley's fist pumped high in the air a tremendous huzzah erupted that brought me more relief than any sound to ever come from man. Enos was alive.

A rope sailed into the stream. Rawley caught it and strong hands pulled them both ashore. They collapsed on the bank and Enos hacked the brown water from his lungs.

But when I finally got to them his eyes found mine. "I was wrong, Pa. Rawley was right. The dam broke just where he said it would. I should have listened to him."

Rawley shook his head. "No, Enos, you were the boss. I should've kept my mouth shut. We couldn't have stopped this anyhow. But now all our gold is gone."

Enos studied the river a bit. "Yeah, but we'll find enough gold to send you to that fancy school. You'll be an engineer. I'll work for you. Together we can build anything."

Rawley's face beamed and he looked up to me. "Does he mean it, Pa?"

"You bet he does." And from deep in my heart I smiled, for the reconciliation of my sons was worth so much more to me than a payback of mere gold could ever be.

The End

– John Putnam

Born and raised in a small South Carolina town John went on to graduate from U.C. Berkeley with a degree in music, but found a laptop keyboard more his forte than a piano. He still lives and works in Berkeley and while researching for his blog, MyGoldRushTales.com, he uncovered his love for the excitement and adventure of the California gold rush.

His first four short stories won story of the month in Frontier Tales. John's first novel, *Hangtown Creek*, sets the scene for his second gold country story in which a pretty girl sweeps young Tom Marsh off his feet and when Tom decides to look for her missing pa he quickly finds himself eyeball to eyeball with the deadliest fiend in the gold country. *Into the Face of the Devil,* was published in 2013 by Pen-L Publishing.

The Lord in This

by Jeff Richards

One day his mother smiles at him over the dining room table. He can see the love sparkle in her eyes like it's something he can touch. The next week she's laid out in a pine-box in the parlor, a frown on her lips. Eyes slammed shut for eternity. Two years later to the month his brother's thrown from a horse. Breaks his neck. Then Cindy Limon goes, the girl he was going to marry, caught in the influenza that roars through town. He is only fourteen and so much bad has happened to him. He figures it's because he was doing something wrong. His mom said, you trust in the Lord, the Lord protect you. You do his bidding, He give you everlasting life. Asa Greer figures that his trust is wearing thin. He needs to work more on his bidding.

That's how he comes to the idea of aiding Reverend Lawrence Wilson who preached about how it is our duty to end the abomination of God.

Asa totes his rifle down the path below the Reverend's house. He puts on a bandana dipped in hog's blood to show he's in the Army of the Lord. He climbs a tree. Hides patiently behind the lush cover of leaves until the light comes on in the preacher's window and he seen Marshall Limon, Cindy's older brother, and Eliot Thomas slink out of the woods to a clearing. Marsh waves a lamp. The light in the window blinks twice. Eliot slinks back in the woods and a few minutes later the runaways slink out with him. Marsh slides down to the river's edge where he uncovers a flatboat beneath a tarp. They all clamber in the boat. Pole across. One of the runaways jumps out when they reach the Ohio side, hugs the ground, and shouts, "The Lord deliver me."

Marsh tells him to hush up. "He ain't delivered you yet."

Two days later, Marsh and Eliot appear on the opposite bank with eight runaways. They pole across. The minister crawls down the hill to greet them. Hugging each of the freed folk in turn. They all crying. Asa wants to leap out of the tree and cry with them, but he knows the Reverend Wilson would send him home. So he stays hidden as a kind of sentinel praying for a chance to prove himself.

That comes one early July twilight a runaway kid breaks through the forest and dives in the water. He ain't much of a swimmer, moving more sideways with the current than forward. But he's half way across when two strangers loop out in the open. Both blond. The one with a goatee carries a gun, the other clean-shaven, hair down to his shoulders. Same blue eyes. Same height. Same slouching demeanor like they was brothers. The clean-shaven one points out the kid flailing in the river. The goateed one shoulders his rifle and fires. The ball plunks in the water a few inches from the runaway's face. The second shot misses entirely and the third hits the kid in the wrist but only seems to hasten his progress across the water. What Asa's thinking is that this ain't much different than the Biblical days. He's heard the song in church, "Oh! Go down, Moses, Away down to Egypt's land." To him those fellows across the river, brothers or not, are like Pharaoh's army and the dark fellow in the river is like the Israelites. Bt there's no parting of waters. Only Asa with his gun and he ain't no Moses. He takes a bead on the goateed blond.

He's a crack shot. Been hunting since he was five. Killed many rabbits. A couple deer and once even a cougar jumped out of a tree near where Tom stood. He caught him in midair. The cougar flopped to the ground harmlessly. Asa saved his brother's life. Only to have it snuffed out when the horse threw him. Where is the Lord in this?

This is what he's thinking as he squeezes the trigger. Sees the sparks. Smells the black powder. Hears the echo from the explosion as it comes back to him like a clap of thunder at the same time he sees a red carnation puff out of the forehead of the goateed blond. The fellow throws out his arms. The rifle flies up in the air end over end. He staggers backward a few steps. Topples to the ground like a tree in the forest. The other blond flinches. Collapses on his knees next to his brother, shakes him but he don't awake. The blond jumps up. Raises his hands to the heavens. Yells a name. Rufus. Skedaddles off to the woods.

Rufus, Asa thinks. That's what you call a dog not a fellow human being. But when he thinks human being, he thinks about what he has done. For a moment he shivers at the thought, then remembers why he done it. His attention skips away from the blond with the red carnation splayed out on the ground. The twilight is fading. The river turns dark though he can see the white ripples of the current as it flows around the rocks near him. He can see a hand reach out of one of the ripples. Clutching the air. Then the hand disappears and he sees a head pop up beyond the rocks.

Asa leaps out of the tree. Stumbles along the embankment. Dives in the water. Swims out to one of the rocks. His eyes dart downstream. He sees no hands. Nor head. Nothing but a wispy, white mist rising from the water. He suspects the current dragged the slave kid under. The river opens up a half mile down. Plunges deeper. He probably sunk to the bottom and they'll find him in a couple of days when he floats up.

On the way home, Asa halts at the cemetery. Whispers a prayer to his brother and Ma. Sidles over to Cindy. The gravestone says,

Cindy Limon
Daughter of John and Sarah
Our Precious Baby
1845-1857

Asa shudders, rubs his eyes. Feels the salty wetness of tears on the back of his hand mixing in with the wetness of the river. He remembers the time they strolled along the bank in the stand of trees where the river widens. The birds singing. Fluttering from tree to tree. He held Cindy's hand. She told him how the teacher kept her after school for slugging Robert Clutch.

"I don't see why," she said. They sat on the ground. Leaned back. Watched a hawk circle the treetops. "Robert pulled my hair. That's why I slugged him."

"You want," Asa whispered. "I'll head over to Robert Clutch's house and beat him up for you. Then I'll throw him in the river."

"You don't have to do that." She laughed. She leaned up on her elbow and kissed Asa on the cheek, her touch as light as a feather duster.

His heart felt like it was about to explode and he couldn't help but profess his love for her.

She wasn't the kind to take things lightly. "Why do you love me?"

"You're beautiful. You're wonderful. You got a tender heart," he said, counting with his fingers. "But most of all, you're as tough as nails like no other woman I ever saw. You won't let no-one push you around."

But he was wrong. God pushed her around.

Asa slogs through the rest of the cemetery with his head down, squeezes between the rails of the wrought iron fence, and slinks past the barn behind his house. The light's out so his daddy's not mending wheels. He's off to the spinster's house. Doesn't give a darn about Asa.

Asa climbs the stairs to his room, pulls off his wet clothes, and jumps in bed. He thinks about the old days when everything was perfect. He thinks about what he has done. Is he justified? Even with the abominations. One time Reverend Wilson preached to the congregation about the slaveholder with his hands dripping in blood, the man who plunders cradles. The man who, to gratify his lust or anger, whips the woman with the lash until the soil is red with her blood. It doesn't matter that the woman is dark-skinned. She is a human being. And you oughtn't to treat human beings like dirt.

Lewis Morgan waits for the fellow in the red bandana to clear the hill by the preacher's house before he slinks out to the clearing. He grabs Rufus by the armpits and drags him in the woods, stopping every few seconds to wipe the tears from his eyes. He stashes him in a hole where a tree had fallen. Covers him with leaves and branches, retrieves the rifle, and stumbles down the path to the road. He races down the road as fast as he can, halting to catch his breath, his mind a complete blank. When he reaches the farmhouse, Lewis creeps up the steps so as not to wake his Ma. Shakes Raymond awake.

"What's a happening?" asks Raymond in a tired voice.

"You must dress. Come downstairs. Something awful to do."

Raymond struggles into his clothes, grumbling the whole time. They creep down the stairs. Outside.

"What the hell so awful you wake me this time of night?" hisses Raymond between his teeth.

Lewis tells him about Rufus.

"What were you doing down there anyways?"

"We planned to go hunting with Duncan. So we looked for him by the cabins, but he wasn't there. But we saw him running down the road and took after him thinking maybe he was playing a game. But when he saw us, he ran faster..."

"That's when you ought to have turned back," says Raymond, shaking his head. "There's people do the chasing for us."

"Well, we didn't," says Lewis, sniffing. He can feel the tears coming on. "We chased him all the way down the road and when we reached the clearing, we saw him in the water. Rufus took some shots at him just to scare him back to our shore and that's when he got himself killed."

"You're a couple of idiots," says Raymond. They hitch the horses to the buckboard and toss a couple blankets in the back. Climb in the seat. Trot off down the road.

When they're far enough away from the house, Lewis yells above the rattle of the buckboard, "I'm sorry, Raymond. I mean it's not like Rufus's our brother or something."

"No, he's our cousin, our Ma's sister's only boy. You realize how upset Ma's going to be, not to speak of Aunt June," says Ray, taking a whip to the horses to make them canter. "Besides Rufus was your best friend. You been hunting together ever since you could handle a gun. And Duncan been going with you. I can't believe you damn fool idiots."

They pull the buckboard off the side of the road. Ray grabs the blankets. Follows his younger brother down the dirt path through the woods. They can see fairly well because the moon's out. A gentle breeze comes up from the river shaking the tree limbs, casting shadows over the path. They hear the sound of twigs snapping in the woods. See a couple deer nibbling the grass next to the fallen tree. The deer run off.

Ray climbs in the hole. Pulls the twigs off and tosses them behind him. He lifts the body. Lewis grabs the legs. They tote Rufus over to the blanket and ease him down.

An animal had torn a hole in his arm. An army of Ants crawls all over the wound.

Lewis runs off to the woods. Leans over. Pukes.

When he drifts back, Ray has covered him with the blanket. "Ain't you seen a corpse before?"

"Sure I have. But that's my friend." He starts to sniffle again.

"Sorry, Buddy." Raymond claps his brother on the shoulder. "I know how you must feel. But it's part your fault."

They lug the body through the woods slowly. It's as heavy as a feedbag. Lewis can't handle the legs because they're stiff as boards and twisted up. His back hurts. It takes his last ounce of energy to flop Rufus on the buckboard. Rufus bounces. The dust flies off him. The blanket folds open, exposes his face. Rufus's eyes are open staring at Lewis, penetrating his skin to what's behind him. He jumps back. Looks around at the gray light spreading across the horizon and at the waning moon. Hears a cock crow nearby.

"I'm scared," he whispers to his brother.

Raymond pulls the blanket over Rufus's face. "Will you stop acting like such a baby?" But he's teary eyed himself and, also, as angry as a cornered barn cat. He guesses nothing will come of this considering the relationship with the people on the other side of the river. He and Lewis'll have to do something themselves. He helps Lewis on the buckboard.

Lewis is thinking about when he, Rufus, and Duncan were kids how they used to play down by the river. Rufus was king. Duncan was the black knight. Lewis the white knight. One time the older boys caught them wearing their wooden swords and capes. Made fun of them. Rufus whacked Raymond in the small of the back. Raymond grabbed Rufus by the cape. Swung him around. Threw him to the ground. Jumped on top of him. The other boys piled on top of Rufus. Lewis and Duncan whacked those boys on their backs until they got distracted. Jumped up. Ran after them. Caught Lewis. Knocked him down. Then it was Rufus and Duncan whacking the boys on the back. It finally ended up that they chased the older boys off. They laughed. Crossed swords. Put their arms around each other. Sang a song they heard when the minstrel show passed through town. About them being the Three Musketeers. "All for one. One for all."

They found the slave boy tangled up in the limbs of a tree that overhung the river and would've thought nothing of it if it wasn't for the gunshot wound to the hand. The sheriff inquired across the river, found that the slave escaped from a farm about three miles up, that two boys chased after him and one of them got murdered by a bullet from the Ohio side of the river. There was an investigation. But nothing came of it.

Asa Greer doesn't feel relief that he hasn't been found out. He doesn't care. He cares for Rufus and the slave kid who lies in the potter's field next to the town drunk. He cares about his eternal soul. But mostly he cares about what he must do next.

One night at the dinner table his Pa announces that he is going to marry the spinster.

"Why you doing that?" asks Asa, leaning across the table. The shadows flicker on his father's face. "Ma wouldn't like it."

"Your Ma's been dead for four years. There's only you and me. And you need someone to take care of you. I can't let you run wild."

"I'm fourteen. I can take care of myself. Besides I don't want that spinster lady to be my ma. She's mean. One time I was crossing her property, she shooed me off with a broom. Nobody likes her."

"She needs a man," says his father, firmly.

Asa clomps upstairs and prays to the Lord. He thinks about when his father marries the spinster, he'll start a family. She isn't that old. Probably twenty-five. Not bad looking. His Pa doesn't need him anymore. He digs around his bureau drawers. Finds the red bandana he hasn't worn since that night. Ties it around his head. Feels the power surge through his whole body like he's been struck by lightning. He thinks of his Ma, his brother, and Cindy Limon and how they are no longer underground in the cemetery but up in Heaven watching his every move. I'll make you proud, he whispers under his breath. He grabs his gun. Tiptoes down the stairs. His father is asleep. He slips outside. Past the barn, through the cemetery, and down the dirt road. Follows the path to the river. He hides.

He waits three days until Marsh Limon and Eliot Thomas appear. They pull the flatboat from behind a clump of reeds. Pole across the river. Hide the boat under the tarp. Disappear in the woods.

Asa strips down to his skivvies. Tosses his clothes, his gun and powder on a couple pieces of driftwood he lashed together. He slides quietly in the water. It is twilight, the sun setting downriver turning the sky a washed out orange color, a line of bright red on the horizon. The trees and river itself seem to have caught fire. Asa kicks upstream around the rocks. Kicks harder when he reaches the main channel. The driftwood turns sideways. Nearly sucks him downstream. He is exhausted when he reaches the Kentucky shore. Crawls out on his hands and knees. Lays back a moment, but he can't wait long least he'll lose Marsh and Eliot. He stands up. Jumps in his clothes. Checks the powder and gun. Dry. I am in the Army of the Lord, he hisses in a low, angry whisper and is about to set off when he hears a twig crack no more than forty feet off. He looks up. Sees two figures saunter out of the woods, one, the shorter of the two, is delicate featured, hair down to the shoulders. The other, who looks to be twenty or so, he doesn't recognize. He's pointing a rifle at Asa's chest. Asa lifts his piece, but before he can finger the trigger, a tongue of fire reaches out from the dark center of the taller one.

Asa Greer staggers back with the impact. Reaches for his chest but doesn't find it. He crashes to the ground, head cocked sideways as though he's listening to the two boys talking as they approach his body.

"Damn, you killed him with one shot," says Lewis Morgan, shaking his head. "You didn't even give me a chance."

"If I gave you a chance," says Raymond Morgan, gently probing Asa's side with the butt of his gun, "it would be one of us is dead. That boy's a crack shot. That is if it is the boy you said shot Rufus."

"It is. I'll swear on a stack of Bibles," says Lewis, raising his hand solemnly. "You see, the bandana."

"Yeah, but anyone can wear a bandana."

"But not anyone with a bandana's going to swim across the river unless he's up to something bad. Like those other two fellows we saw. You know what they're up to."

"I don't know anything for sure," says Raymond. "Now you stop your jabbering. We got to get rid of this body before someone comes along."

    They toss Asa's gun as far out in the river as they can. Kick the driftwood off shore. Then roll Asa down the embankment until he plops in the water. They push him off and watch as he slides downriver, his head still above water as if he's looking up at the orange sky at a hawk circling lazily around and around like in a dream.

The End

– Jeff Richards'

fiction and essays have appeared in more than two-dozen publications such as *Prick of the Spindle, Pinch, New South*, and *Southern Humanities Review* and four anthologies including *Stress City* (Paycock Press). He has recently completed a novel in short story form about his relatives who fought in the Civil War called *Open Country* and is looking for a publisher. Three of the stories from his novel have appeared in *Frontier Tales*, one in the anthology *Filtered Through Time*, and one forthcoming in *Gargoyle*.

Richards lives with his wife and Bichon in Takoma Park, Maryland, a mile from Fort Stevens, a Civil War battle site. He is a blues music fanatic and is presently writing blues stories that he hopes also to make into a book. Two of these stories have been published. Finally Richards is building a theme blog called *Side-kick Review* where he plans to feature his own writing as well as others. "The Lord in This" is based on the Rankin House in Ripley, Ohio where over 2000 slaves escaped across the Ohio River to freedom.

CAYO BRADLEY

by Nina Romano

A whistle sleek as moonlit grass captured the attention of Darby McPhee. She listened to the remains of its sibilance with longing, wanting to run away. How long could she stay in that cottage slaving away her youth for her five brothers and father? Darby was days shy of her fifteenth birthday when the three o'clock whistle blew. She'd made up her mind. Tomorrow she'd be on that iron panther heading for the east, her Aunt Bea's, an education and a new life.

There were several obstacles she'd have to overcome not the least of them the fact she might never return. She would take her courage in her two hands, like her Pa told her so many times to do when she faced a fearful thing and she'd tell Cayo Bradley just how she felt about him. And it would be today. Wondering what it would be like to kiss him, she rolled up her sleeves.

Darby reached for the butter churn and poured in the cream she had skimmed off the milk. Her thoughts followed the white stream. Then veered with, *After all, I may never see him again, and a man ought to know if he's been loved, even if it's a starry-far-away love that can never be fulfilled.* Her anger and fear were felt in every forceful slam of the stick with its round flat disk end. She'd make butter all right and she'd cream away every worry and dang thought about the long train ride east, leaving Pa and telling Cayo. What if he didn't feel the same? Wouldn't matter, she'd be leaving anyway. And a man should know.

Darby rushed to finish her chores. She set the table, pulled the muffins from the oven, turned the bacon, and whisked a dozen eggs with farm cheese she'd made earlier that morning. Standing in the doorway, she clanged an iron triangle, calling the men to breakfast. When will I tell Pa? She patted the pocket of her apron, which held Aunt Bea's letter stating all the arrangements she'd made for her niece. Darby slapped the butter onto a daisy form cut-out made of an oval piece of sorrel wood, closed the three inch high wooden mold with scalloped edges around it and hooked a curved nail over the head of another nail to secure it. She ran to the barn giving a hoot to her eldest brother Garret and buried the butter shape under the ice protected by hay. It always amazed her how the hay kept the blocks of ice from melting, but this would be the last time she'd have to concern herself about farm things like this. Aunt Bea had an ice box. City folk lived so much better.

The omelets were made and served. Garret reached for the strawberry preserves that Darby put up last summer.

"Pa, pass the biscuits," Garrett said. "Hey, girl, where's the butter?"

"I've a given name, Garret, just like you," she said. "I'll get it. I put it to cool in the barn."

"Probably just cuddling that dumb old sheep dog is all," Darby's father said.

"Not," Darby muttered and walked out the kitchen door.

Garret and Pa. She'd miss them. The only ones who recognized the fact that she was the opposite sex. Darby's younger brothers, Bixby, Randy, Chad and Pat, were inconsiderate. Darby thought of them as irresponsible assholes. Pa and Garret were always at them to fix something they'd messed up. Or to get going on a task or chore that should have been finished days before. Lazy bunch of oafs, serve them right to have to clean up after themselves.

When Darby came back from the barn the sun was full up.

"Can't you read?" she asked the men.

"Sure," said Pa. He pushed away from the table and was about to light a cigarette he'd just rolled.

"Pa, out of respect for your dead wife and my Momma, please don't smoke in the house," Darby said. She took hold of a sign she'd made. It was pinned to the gingham curtain on the window nearest the big oak dining table where her family sat.

She read, "Close the shades when the sun is full up."

Darby let the curtain fall and closed the shade. Then she picked up a sign that was leaning on a milk bottle used as a vase for wild flowers.

"More stink weeds in this house than milk," said her younger brother Pat.

"Hush up," she said. And she read from her second note. "It says here, pick up your dish and bring it to the kitchen, or you can eat off the unwashed, doggone thing, oink oink, next meal."

She tossed the note on the table and began clearing away the breakfast remains.

"Skinny as a broomstick, child. You eat?" Pa asked.

"Sure, Pa, at three o'clock when I got up to start my chores." Now's my chance. "I've got a letter from Aunt Bea. Been meaning to let you read. I'll set it by the wash bucket."

"I'll have a look see when I come in at sundown," said Pa.

Thank Heavens. "I have to rush now. Mrs. Miller expects me at the store early today, it being Saturday. There'll be lots of farmer wives and hands coming in for supplies," Darby said to her father who'd caught her around the waist and gave her a squeeze. She felt a twinge of guilt. Looking at her father, she thought of a dozen kindnesses he'd gone out of his way to do for her. She'd miss him, but she couldn't sacrifice her life any longer. Momma's been gone five years. It goes by all too quickly, and I'm not his wife.

At times Darby felt like a mother hen to his sons. That was a thing her father would have to reckon with when she left.

Darby had mulled this over in her mind many times. But the day before her departure it was a tune that was wearing itself out. Momma's dead, not coming back and I'm leaving, Pa. This time I'm really going.

Chad had gone out and come back in. He was holding a piece of paper in his hand. "Hear ye, hear ye. I found this note nailed to the outhouse door in Darby's scratchy hand. Says: Throw in lye after each deposit."

Everyone laughed. And Darby went to the kitchen to do the dishes. A note meant for the boys, said, Always, prime the pump. They'll get on just fine.

That dusty summer of 1873 found Cayo Bradley working as a hired hand and sometime cowpoke on the Lindstrom ranch in Parcel Bluffs. Cayo never had a day off, but Saturday afternoons he'd hitch up the wagon for Libby and Mrs. Lindstrom and take them to town. Libby was nothing like her friend Darby. The Lindstrom girl was spoiled and arrogant and Cayo overheard Darby once tell Libby that her Daddy ought to give his darling daughter a once-and-for-all-time good licking to straighten her skinny ass out. Mr. Lindstrom had tossed Cayo a full pouch of chewing tobacco for the ride to town. Cayo guessed it was the old man's way of thanking him for putting up with his daughter. But all his boss had said was, "Watch the ruts and gopher holes, Cayo, and have a high time, ladies."

The Lindstrom women would go visiting at the parlor in Hotel Ryder, drink tea, and, with tongues as sharp as scissors, cut to pieces every other woman in town. Sometimes they would go to the dressmaker Fanny Oates, or tend to some other womanly tasks. Lastly, before they headed home they would stop into Fern and Harris Miller's General Store where Darby McPhee worked as a salesgirl.

The Millers were childless. Fern was able to handle the regular trade during weekdays, but on Saturdays and Sundays things were hectic because the farm folk turned up in town to replenish their stores. Darby was hired to take up the slack and deal with the weekend rush. Fern was a motherly figure for Darby and tried to draw the girl out. She was partially responsible for Darby's decision to leave Parcel Bluffs for educational greener pastures in the east with Aunt Bea.

Cayo Bradley was a lean man with sharply cut cheekbones and bronze skin. Some said he was part Apache. Others claimed he was left for dead by bandoleros, and because of his mean disposition, not even the coyotes would go near him. Maybe that's where he got his name. Nobody in town knew him by any other. Whatever his component parts were, it was for certain he was a man quick with a Bowie knife, swifter with a whip. He wore chaps every day but Saturday when he drove the buckboard. Cayo carried a Colt pistol in his holster and never rode his horse without a Winchester rifle strapped to his saddle. He was a man that people respected, a man who kept his mouth shut and eyes peeled, even the eyes they said he had in the back of his head.

On Main Street, Cayo would stop and talk a spell with Sheriff Link Jones. He rode posse for Link when the train had been held up the year before. Link didn't care if Cayo was a man with a past or not. All Link knew for certain was that Cayo could draw fast, shoot sure, ride and rope better than any damn cowhand he'd seen since his own father died. And because Cayo joined last year's posse, Link was able to apprehend Bick McAlister and his brother Greer. But Cayo wanted no part of the lynching, and, afterward, when he was offered Bick's new tooled boots, he refused.

Cayo would stroll to the bath house and have a shave and bath, paying his two bits, with a thumb snap underneath, flip-ping the coin in the air for the owner Sara Birch. Trim and tidy, he'd meander over to Miller's General Store flanked by a telegraph-assay office on one side and a bank on the other.

When Cayo opened the door to the general store and stepped inside he was surprised at the cool dank air that hit him. Like a cellar. The next thing he sensed was the autumn rich smell of dried apples. When his eyes became accustomed to the dark, then he noticed, almost tripped on, a keg of dried fruit. He began to make out clear images. Not in the least was the tall, straight young body of Darby McPhee. She was standing behind a counter. The shelves and wood planks behind her were beautiful intricate patterns of flowers, deer, and mountain goats. The carvings were disarmingly graceful patterns straight out of the mountains of Bavaria designed by the capable chipping and scaling of the carpenter Heinz Schroeder. The shelves were lined with Mason Jars of peaches preserved in thick syrup, and glasses of homemade raspberry, blueberry, blackberry and strawberry jams, covered with wax. There were tins of black strap molasses, hurricane lanterns with extra long wicks, boxes of four inch wooden sulphur matches and bottles of tomatoes.

On the counter were burlap sacks of strange spices marked with names like oregano, basil, peppercorns, marjoram, sage, rosemary, thyme and dill. On the floor in front of the counter were larger gunnysacks of white beans, rice, lentils, cane sugar, flour and cornmeal.

Darby said, "Say, Cayo."

Cayo tipped his hat. "How do?"

"Tickety-boo." She smiled her father's smile.

Cayo looked about and seeing the owner absent asked after her. "And Miss Fern?"

"Over to the tinsmith. You needing something beside your shirt? Need tobacco? Special blend costs five cents a pouch, but this here one's just as sweet and it's a penny."

It was like there were no other customers in the place the way she looked at him. Not yet fifteen, but a woman made.

"Make it a penny worth. He walked up to the counter and extended his doe-skin pouch.

She deals with all these cackling hens, boisterous drunks. Cooks and cleans for her Pa and five nasty suckers she calls brothers. She loves me. I feel it. Know it. She takes extra care of me spending too much. And here again. He watched Darby as she folded his ironed shirt and started wrapping it in brown paper.

"Hold on," Darby said, "Let me tend this first so's it don't smell like tobacco."

Cayo put a five cent piece and a penny on the counter.

"Too much," she said. "Only one cent for work shirts. Five's for dress ones, if they's got ruffles."

Was she saving me money here, too? She could charge what she liked. Fern Miller let Darby take in ironing and she made her own prices. Cayo's face flushed and he was glad of the darkness, and the cooler inside air. He switched a penny, taking up the Shield nickel from the counter. Opening his pouch, he waited. Not just for chewing tobacco. For what? I'm fifteen years her senior, yet when I see her I'm a dunce of twelve. He looked at his hands, the palms began to sweat. He wiped his hands on his pants.

When I'm at the spread I think of things I'm going to tell her—how a calf is all warm when he's born, and after—how he's all wet with his momma's juices. The thanks in the mother's eyes when you've helped pull her baby free. What it feels like to rope a steer, and how the air smells when you burn his flesh with a branding iron. I can tell her of the high full moon over the prairie and stars you can touch with all the shooting arches of light that make you think there's another universe somewhere out yonder. And here I'm wanting to give her cornflowers and buttercups and Libby's bell-shaped tiny lilies of the valley. Tell her I'd like to have her for my own. To smell the skin of her, to wake up to her tousled hair on my pillow and arm. There's that knot again in my stomach. If I don't eat Johnnycake for a year I wouldn't go and miss it. But it ain't corn bread, it's when can I tell her? And how do I?

Darby's fingertips barely touched Cayo's. They looked at each other. Long and hard. She drew her hand away as if she had all day to do that one thing.

Then she turned her back and started putting things on the shelves and said, "I'm home bound at four o'clock today. I take the back path by the old curved road. It's earlier than I usually leave."

Why's she telling me this?

Darby faced him, dusted the counter of the spilled tobacco with her apron and said, "I'll be doing some packing and such besides preparing supper for the boys and Pa. Tell Libby for me I'll ride by later around eight. They'll be finished eating then, won't they?"

Cayo stood there like a storefront Indian. A wooden statue had more life. He felt no blood course through his veins. Time stood still. She's leaving. Leaving Parcel Bluffs. Leaving me. Without ever having told her how I feel about her.

"Can I walk you home, Darby?"

"It's a ways, Mr. Cayo Bradley, but I'd be pleased of the company. And ... " she pulled her hair behind her ears, and gulped some air, "and there's something I've been meaning to say to you."

A customer came in with two small children. Cayo held the door for the woman.

"Yeah, me too," Cayo said, tipped his hat, and walked out.

Libby Lindstrom knew how Darby felt about Cayo. Libby had hoped that Cayo felt the same way about her, not Darby. But somehow she knew he cared only for Darby. He was in love or desire or whatever with Darby McPhee, her best friend since forever.

Libby noticed how at times when she talked to him how he'd get that far look in his eye, and be someplace else. Mind traveling she called it. But at the mention of Darby's name, his pointy ears'd prick up and his nostrils wriggled—a coyote who'd caught a scent.

There were other things. Little things. Libby couldn't define surely, but the signs were there for anyone interested enough to read them. And she was interested. Now her dear friend and foe would be leaving on the train east tomorrow. The night before Libby hadn't slept well with the excitement of Darby's parting and the possibility of taking hold of Cayo's lonesome heart. Darby's secret was the one thing she kept to herself. She'd been a chatterbox all the way to town.

"Woodpeckers make less fuss with their morning tapping. The buckboard noise seems quiet compared to you, Libby. Hush now you're bringing on one of my migraines," Mrs. Lindstrom said, fiddling with an empty bottle of laudanum through the cloth of her purse.

Libby wasn't sure, but could swear Cayo smirked. It seemed to her that he was keeping the corners of his mouth controlled as they worked to turn upwards. Thunderation and damnation. What do I see in him anyway he's so ornery and mean-tempered? He could look under my skirt and still never crack loose with a smile. I hate him forever. Well, till tomorrow anyway.

At Mrs. Ryder's social tea, Libby didn't join in with the usual catty talk of the women. Instead she sulked, got up and looked out the window, her mind calculating the whereabouts of Cayo Bradley. He always went to the Miller's for stores, but who knew just when.

Libby didn't want to give the lovers a chance to declare their rightful feelings for each other. She wanted to ruin the bitter-sweet departure—a probable promise of letters and a future meeting.

Probably die and go straight to hell, I will, trying to break up something right as raindrops on windflowers.

"I declare," Mrs. Ryder said to Mrs. Lindstrom, pouring tea

into a porcelain cup, "your gal's a might quiet today."

"Thank the Almighty," said Mrs. Lindstrom. "Libby was a mockingbird on our way into town." She lifted the honey pot and heaped a generous spoonful into the steaming brew.

"Mrs. Ryder, Ma, I'll take leave now and get a breath of air; maybe set a spell with Darby over to Miller's. It's always cooler there."

"You do look a bit peaked. You all right?" Suddenly there was a note of concern in Mrs. Lindstrom's voice.

"Um-hum," said Libby. "Really. Fine."

She walked out the door listening to her mother call her a flibbertigibbet, and worst tempered-soul the Savior ever put in Parcel Bluffs. "Why the only person who can hold rein on that girl is Cayo Bradley."

"That so?" Mrs. Ryder asked as Libby closed the door.

She sauntered her most genteel walk over to Miller's, every now and again using her parasol as a walking stick. On the walk to Miller's, she dwelt on how the conversation would go with Darby, and what she could buy as a pretext for walking in without her mother. Rock candy.

Libby hadn't timed her visit right. Instead of Cayo, Darby was waiting on a different cowboy. When Darby finished, she turned and excused herself to Fern Miller. Libby heard Darby say, "I need to have a moment's privy, to tend something personal, if it'd be all right?"

Fern said, "Sure thing."

Darby and Libby stepped into the back storeroom behind a curtain and perched themselves on a bale of cotton. As if by ritual both girls fanned themselves with their smocks.

"Did you get my message?" asked Darby.

"What message?"

"I told Cayo to tell you I'd be over after your supper tonight to say my farewells."

"Cayo was here already? Where'd he go to?"

"Mighty interested in a hired hand, Libby. Thought you'd be caring to hear the particulars of my departure east."

"Sure I am. It's just that I'm surprised."

They put down their aprons and smoothed the folds.

"Surprised at what?"

"He came in so early."

"Snooping, huh? He always comes for his ironing. Today he came ahead of time cause he's plum out of chewing tobacco."

"That's untrue, Darby McPhee."

"You calling me a liar? What's got into you? The man bought chewing—"

"He couldn't chomp a pouchful in two hours." Libby fidgeted with her hands.

"The pouch was empty." Darby stressed the last word.

"I saw Daddy fling a small bulging purse to him this very morning."

"We're arguing over something real dumb, you know that? Hold on just one tinker's damn."

"No need to curse."

"Why you're jealous, and flushing red. Got a hankering for your Daddy's ranch hand, now don't you, little Miss Libby Lindstrom?"

"Not—"

"That's a sin of covetousness. You know how I feel about him. Known forever. Out the sky drops a hawk, no a vulture. Some friend." Darby jumped off the bale. "You could have leastwise had the decency to wait till I was snug-as-a-bug-in-a-rug tucked in at Aunt Bea's."

"Did you tell him your feelings yet?"

Darby put her hands on her hips and swayed slightly. "Now that's for me to know and you to find out. None of your concern. And forget the message. I won't be riding out to see you tonight or ever."

At four o'clock sharp, Darby said goodbye to Harris and Fern Miller. She thanked Harris and kissed Fern, then put her pay in her pocket. Cayo Bradley slouched against the back wall of the General Store, his hat pulled low over his eyes. He tipped it back and stood up straight before Darby's hand touched the door.

Darby walked outside and immediately shielded her eyes. As soon as they adjusted to the brightness, she dropped her hand. She wanted Cayo to take hold of it, but knew he wouldn't even if he was dying to. How to begin?

For the first fifteen minutes she began but faltered, trying to make small talk. He took up where she left off, his efforts were more clumsy and more endearing.

Sagebrush rolled across the path. Mountains surrounded them. Scrub pines, yucca and thistles covered the dry patchwork of red earth. Cattails and wild iris interspersed goldenrod.

Cayo linked his thumbs in the belt loops of his pants and Darby walked with her arms in back of her, right hand grasping her left thumb.

She stopped to pick a piece of prairie grass and kept on walking as she chewed the flat blade till it gave up the last of its juices. Then she tossed it, watching the slight breeze glide it to the ground. Kite to the right, she thought. She stopped again in the middle of the path.

"I've been meaning to tell you about my Aunt Bea back east."

"Don't think I want to hear if it's to do with them bags you'll be packing."

"I lack book learning. Need to get away from my brothers. I'll miss Pa, but he'll get on, and before you know it I'll be back in Parcel Bluffs—"

"They ain't no such thing as coming home. Once a critter leaves the nest, he gets a taste for flying high. Things look mighty different from up there."

"How'd you know? You a bird?"

"I been a bird sometimes in Indian country. I've tasted ground herbs make you fly like a feathered arrow, make you know life from inside an eagle."

Darby and Cayo continued walking, shoulders almost touching. "What's it like?"

"Like to bust out your skin, or hold on tight to a girl. Never let go, if'n that girl be you."

Darby looked sidewards but was afraid to stop walking, kicking up little squalls of dust for fear she'd never recapture this moment. But she had to look at him, see the moonless night of his eyes.

Darby stood dead still in her tracks. Cayo put his hands in his pockets and shrugged his shoulders. She hesitated a minute then said, "I think of you sometimes ... when I'm pitching hay, or milking, or rag-washing the kettles, or dusting Momma's Bible." Darby brushed back the hair off her face. "Even with my eyes open, looking at something else, I see you."

Cayo spat the rest of his chewing tobacco through his teeth. "I've seen you in the cottonwoods when I was flying over," he said pointing to the sky. "Even before I knowed it were you. I saw the black panther riding east. But you was churning butter. In Indian country." Cayo pulled out his tobacco pouch, looked at it, put it back in his pocket.

Darby's eyes followed his movements, remembered the feel of the doeskin and beadwork she'd touched just a few hours ago. Who had made it for him? "Libby came to Miller's after you left. She told me her Daddy gave you a pouch this morning."

"That be true. I gave it to Link Jones. Don't cotton to gifts with tie strings, makes a man indebted." He heaved a sigh. "Miss Libby. Well, now, she's got some real learning to do. She ain't no Darby McPhee."

Darby felt her cheeks get hot. The McPhee ranch was in sight. Cayo took Darby's hand in his and squeezed the fingertips gently. They walked to the shade of a pinon tree on top of a bluff. The whole valley lay before them like a penny postcard. Darby leaned against the tree. They stood inches apart. Cayo rested his hand on the trunk just above her shoulder.

"I ain't much with words, Darby, but I got lots of feelings. If you want, I'll talk to your Pa. Tonight if you say, and you can pack your duds, but, not to travel east, to set up house with me."

Darby looked a little frightened and puzzled, until Cayo added, "It'd be a proper wedding with a preacher. You tell me if and when you're a wanting to get hitched.

He put his other hand up above her shoulder.

Bird in a cage.

"I'll be heading back up there." He nudged his chin in the direction of the Sangre de Cristos Mountains. "Soon as the summer corn's in. Got a cabin needs a woman's hands to give it warmth.

"I was banking on learning to be a teacher." She heard herself hedge.

He took hold of both her hands.

"I can help nature teach you things ain't in no books. You can school your own kids. Ours. Time I was settling in, Darby."

Darby listened, her heartbeat pulsing faster with every word he stammered on. Her mind raced. No fair asking a man to wait. And me afraid he wouldn't want me. But he does. Darby grew so still, she thought he'd hear the pounding in her chest.

Finally she said, "I never been east, nor seen the ocean." But the deep of his eyes'll be forever.

She reached up to grasp his hands.

"You'll glimpse it all when our baby calls you in fright cause he climbed a perch too tall, and you catch him in your arms."

"Lots of folks never go east or travel to the sea." She took a deep breath and blurted out, "I can't chance leaving you to make high-cheeked babies with the likes of Libby Lindstrom."

Cayo smiled a small smile.

Darby returned the smile. "Got some yellow gingham I was

fixing to sew into curtains."

"Yellow'd be mighty pretty on them cabin windows. What do you say, Darby?"

"If that's a proposal, Cayo Bradley, my answer's yes, but I best get home afore Pa sees Aunt Bea's letter."

"I'll come round to talk to your Pa at 8."

"Make it 7:30? Got to telegraph Aunt Bea to come west."

Time sped to no time. Before she could even dream it, Cayo took hold of Darby's sun-warmed arms and clasped them around his neck. She closed her eyes and tilted up her chin. But the second Cayo covered her lips with his, she opened her eyes. A kiss for all times.

A kiss to remember.

The End

– Nina Romano

earned a B. S. degree from Ithaca College, an M.A. from Adelphi University and a B. A. and M.F.A. in Creative Writing from Florida International University. She lived in Rome, Italy, for twenty years where many of her poems and stories are set. She is fluent in Italian and Spanish.

Romano has been an intern and assistant at the Palm Beach Poetry Festival to Marie Howe, Denise Duhamel, and CK Williams. She has facilitated poetry and creative writing workshops at the Ft. Lauderdale Main Library, the Sanibel Island Writers Conference, Bridle Path Press Baltimore, Lopez Island Library, Florida Gulf Coast University, Rosemary Beach and the Outreach Program of Palm Beach Poetry Festival.

Her short fiction, memoir and poetry appear in numerous reviews and literary journals. Excerpts from her novel-in-progress, *The Secret Language of Women*, appear in *Dimsum: Asia's Literary Journal, Southern Women's Review* and *Driftwood*.

Romano has been nominated twice for a Pushcart Prize. She has authored three poetry collections: *Cooking Lessons* by Rock Press and submitted for a Pulitzer Prize, and *Coffeehouse Meditations,* from Kitsune Books, and *She Wouldn't Sing at My Wedding* from Bridle Path Press. She has co-authored *Writing in a Changing World.*

Her debut short story collection, *The Other Side of the Gates* and her newest collection of poetry, Faraway Confections are forthcoming. More about Nina Romano at www.ninaromano.com

A Saddle in the Desert

by Tom Sheehan

He was in the sparse land between shifting sands of the great desert and the last tree bearing green when he saw the vultures descending from their high flight. Breward Chandler, "Brew" to friends back in the mountains where breathing was much easier than here in the midst of little life, sat bareback on an Indian pony he had freed from a natural corral behind a blow-down. Chandler had learned that the horse would obey pulls on his mane and in this manner he had escaped from sure capture by heading into the desert, with his pistols loaded and a lariat and a canteen he had grabbed on the run. He was not sure who was after him, either renegade Indians or renegade whites out for the kill, looking for guns, clothes, saddles, anything for free. He was hoping that they'd measure the little he might have against the rigors of a chase in the desert. Perhaps, he also hoped, they were smarter than he thought they were.

The canteen was almost empty and water had to be found.

Now, arrowed out of the high sky, he saw the vultures drop down and out of sight ahead of him. There was no hesitation on his part; he'd have to check the attraction. It might only be a natural desert kill, but it could be a man caught in the last tremors of life and death, a man like him, on the run from one thing or another. It was easy to see that life was full of such chases; he was proof of it.

He dipped into a slight swale, crested a small hill as much

dune as he had imagined, and saw the horde of black birds at the carcass of a horse, the saddle in place. Chandler, watching them feast on the horse's flesh, stayed in place, now and then looking back over his shoulder for signs of any pursuit.

In less than half an hour the vultures had almost stripped the bones of flesh. Hoping they had done little damage to the saddle, he galloped in on the hungry critters and drove them off. Shortly they were aligned again high overhead on the lift of a thermal, like people waiting to get into church or for a general store to open its doors.

To his everlasting thanks, the saddle was undamaged and did not take him long to get it off the carcass remnants and onto the pony. The pony, not surprising Chandler, did not like the smell of death that came upon him, but he held the pony in place by hobbling his front legs.

The saddle looked to be a good old Texas saddle, with a high back, one that would have lasted the rider for life, wherever he was. Or if he was. The initials LGT were burned into the pommel textured into the skirts, and the whole rig showed a few years of use. He'd have to look for the owner, see if he had fallen off, had been wounded, died of thirst. He could not tell how the horse had died. He assumed that if the rider was dead out there some-where the vultures would have gone after him also.

Chandler only agreed that he would search ahead of him on the trail for the owner, not behind him, not wanting to run into those chasing him, or had been chasing him. The desert, he wished again, might hold them back.

When he rode off, sitting comfortable at last on the pony, the vultures returned to their feeding, and no signs of pursuit appeared on the wide horizon. Chandler figured his pursuers had backed off because of the desert threats. Ahead of him, near the Barracks Rim, sat a waterhole the old Kiowa, Bent Wing, had told him about earlier in time, the night they had sat outside Knock's Tavern at the junction of three trails in the mountains.

Knock himself had introduced Chandler to Bent Wing, saying, "Listen to all he says, son. He knows more than any ten mountain men I know. He knows mountain and desert, grass and foothills, forest and canyon, like no one else does. And it's all free for you. I saved his life one time and he ain't never forgot it. No sir, not Bent Wing, Kiowa of all Kiowas. You mark every word he says. And he says things that will matter to you sometime down the trail, where things happen to a man the way they have for a thousand years out here, and he knows it all. Count on it. Came down to him from all the shamans that come before him, loading him up."

Knock had shaken his finger right in Chandler's nose at the end of that discussion; "Don't think him an old Indian blowing steam, boy. Just realize what he says will save your life someday. He ain't talking for nothing, he's talking good 'cause he's still trying to pay me back, being good to friends of mine."

Through Chandler's mind went the location of half a dozen waterholes in the range of the desert. The markers came back to him from his lessons at the tent of the Kiowa that one night outside Knock's Tavern. "One water hole is like a breath of air in the desert, and sits near the Barracks Rim where the old fort used to be. The elder of all shamans told me it runs a thousand feet underground to cleanse itself for thirsty men. Comes clear through the mountain from a high lake the great god made."

Bent Wing told him about more water holes the Kiowa gods had sent to his tribe. "We share what has been given to us. You must do the same."

"Have any of them gone dry?"

"Oh, many. Those that were hidden from a decent thirst were fired dry by an angry god. No man owns a water hole."

Land marks had been explained to him by Bent Wing, places to look for, to look from, measures to be made, marks that were left for Indian eyes now coming to his eyes. The eagle talon on the face of a rock as he closed on Barracks Rim told him the waterhole was close enough to grasp. He found the slit of water at the base of Barracks Rim, in a cluster of rocks. In half an hour he had filled his canteen. The water had appeared in a slit of rock and disappeared in the rock cluster not pooling up at all. He had never seen one like it, and was thankful the old Kiowa had shared its location with him.

As Chandler prepared to leave he caught sight of a flash of sunlight reflected from a surface down the trail ahead of him. It flashed again and then it flashed again. A minute later it flashed again.

Someone was signaling him. Chandler looked down at the initials on the saddle, thinking he had found the saddle owner, that he had found LGT.

Chandler urged the pony toward the flashing source, perhaps a mile away. Behind him there appeared to be no pursuit, and under him the saddle, LGT's saddle, was new to him but comfortable in a few strides of the Indian pony. With nothing behind him, Chandler wondered what was in front of him. Would he find LGT up there with the reflections, obvious signals for help? If it was the owner of the saddle, he'd be riding bareback again. Perhaps soon.

Perhaps not. The place of the signals he had marked by an overhanging outcrop, a bulge that Bent Wing would have attributed to the Great God pushing on the earth, making new places, new gardens, new forests, and, of course, to test man, new deserts.

From a hundred feet away he saw the man's arm swing slowly, the way a tired man swings his arm or a wounded man. Chandler, approaching with caution, knew from about ten feet that the man was wounded. Blood was all over his shirt, one arm solely red. It was not the arm he had waved.

"I'm glad to see you, mister. I thought I'd never get another drink of water. I'm bone dry, near dead, but want a drink of water." Then, after looking at the pony, he said, "I see you found my saddle."

"You LGT?"

With his finger pointing at Chandler's canteen, he said, "Yes, Lorne Taylor. I'm from the Barrel Ranch, the Bar-Circle-B. Got jumped by some renegades and galloped down this way hoping they wouldn't chase me. But a round caught me square from a long way off and I crawled in here as my horse ran off. Must have been hit too."

"What's the G for?"

"Gawaian. My father brought it from Australia a long time ago. It's a native name, like he wanted to hold onto something. He jumped ship on the west coast. Was a sailor and became a herder. Had enough of the sea."

Chandler held the canteen as Taylor took a small sip, then a gulp. "Sorry for taking your water, but it's a swap ... you got my saddle." He tried to laugh, but it didn't come out right. He coughed deeply.

"My pals will be looking for me," he said. "If they find you with my saddle you better be able to explain in a hurry why you have it. I can't be any clearer than that. They'll look for me until they find me, no matter what shape I'm in."

He coughed again, and this time it was deep and sounded as if it was not going to let go of him.

He waited until he caught his breath, and Chandler knew he was in the presence of a tough, tough man, who said, "If I had a pencil and paper I'd write you a bill of sale, my saddle for the best drink of water I ever had, but I haven't got them. If they catch up to you tell them my middle name. That'll be proof enough that I gave it to you. I won't make it out of here, I know that. Tell them my last thoughts find them doing what they like best. You have to swear to that,"

"I swear," Chandler said. "I swear." He raised his hand.

Taylor began a small litany. "One's a singer and writes his own songs, plays great guitar. One would rather fish than anything in the world and then eat the catch at an open fire. He's a dreamer, but a worker like the others. One's a lover, enough said. But they're all good men on a drive. We've been together for a long time. Since we were half a knee high. Be careful, though; they can be impulsive when one of us has been hurt or misjudged or even called a bad name out of turn, the likes of which have started a minor brawl or two in a few saloons."

Besides the coughing, Chandler knew other things were working down in Taylor. His face grimaced several times, the way one might measure the onslaught of different pains, how deep they went, how long they lasted.

"What are their names?" Chandler said.

Taylor, about to speak, held one hand up in a pause, took a noisy, deep breath, shook, looked at Chandler right in the eyes, and died on the spot. Blood ran from his mouth in one gush, and stopped, as if the whole mechanism of the body quit on the spot after a final shiver and shake that ran down his frame.

Always looking around him for signs of danger, checking out every swirl of dust, Chandler assembled enough rocks and stones and limestone slabs at the foot of the rim to inter LG Taylor from the ravages of animals and vultures. The only mark he left was scratched into the face of the cliff ... LGT. A good eye would be able to see the letters.

Taylor's hat, a good Stetson, became Chandler's, but he left Taylor's boots in place, burying them with the man under the pile of rocks. He did not want to step into the other man's boots, plain and simple. The Good Words were spoken over the site and Chandler, with renewed spirit, set off again.

Late in the day, after drifting across an arid stretch of land, he found a break in the cliff face and started the climb to the top of Barracks Rim. At the top, after an arduous trip even for the Indian pony, he was in an instant surrounded by five riders.

"We heard you coming up, mister, so we just waited." The speaker not only sounded mean, he looked mean, as he said,

"Tell me where you got that saddle, mister. And you better be clean and quick about it." His hands bore two Smith & Wesson shooters, aimed right at Chandler. "Say it all slow, mister, but say it all."

"The saddle was given to me by a man named Lorne Taylor. I found him wounded down below the rim. He said he was chased by some renegades though he wasn't sure if they were Indians or what. I think it might have been the same ones who chased me, got my horse."

"Where'd you get the pony?"

"He was trapped in the corner of a canyon by a blow-down that cut his escape route. I had to break his way out of there. Those who were chasing me went right past the blow-down and the pony kept quiet. But they might still be after me."

"So where's this Taylor fella you're talking about?"

"I buried him down below the rim. Marked the wall with his initials, like on his saddle. See, LGT there." He pointed down at the skirt of the saddle.

"Maybe you killed him. How does that sound? How do we know you ain't lying about it all? Even making up the story about him giving you his saddle. Where's his horse?"

"Gone to vulture food," Chandler replied. "I saw it straight off. They dropped in on the horse like they were shot at it. Half the animal gone when I came close on them."

"Where was the rider?"

"I got the saddle off and put it on the pony and a bit later I saw some flashing from the base of the rim. That's where I found Taylor, been shot bad. Said he'd write me a bill of sale for the saddle, but had no pencil."

The reply was still mean. "You could have made it all this up."

"Told me his pards would come. Told me about them. The singer. The lover. The fisherman. That you boys?"

"You could have heard that from anybody who knows us. None of it is secret. We don't know if we'll believe you or not. You

got his hat." He looked down at Chandler's boots after he checked the Stetson. "Where's his boots?"

"On him when I buried him. I didn't need them, but I didn't
have a hat."

"Anything else?"

"Told me what "G" stands for."

"Oh, yah, what for?"

"Said his daddy brought it all the way from Australia when he
jumped ship on the coast. Stands for Gawaian, some native
name."

"That's okay with us then. You sound like you treated Lorne
square. Let's see where you buried him. We have to say our words
for him. He was a good cowpoke, a good friend to all of us. We'll
miss him. We'll miss him a lot."

He shifted in the saddle, looked at his pals and said, "Let's
take care of this and then tomorrow we'll chase down those
coyotes. We'll need a horse for this fella. What's your name,
mister?"

"Breward Chandler. No middle initial. They call me Brew. I
was on my way to a new job in Parkersville."

"For now, Brew, you got another new job."

They all started back down the trail, through the break in the
rim, with Chandler in the lead. They were just about at the
bottom when he threw up his hand after he had spotted movement back along the base of the cliff. It was not more vultures
but half a dozen riders just about where he had covered Taylor
with rocks.

One by one the new friendship team slipped into a low break
in the land, and moved half way to the group of men working at
the burial site.

They were disinterring LG Taylor.

Without a signal of any kind, like a single mind was working,
the men charged at the men at the site. The battle did not last
long. And one man lived long enough to tell them who he and

his pards worked for, and why.

Chandler, as it turned out, was no longer just along for the ride ... he had become one of them, and sat the saddle that had always had been part of them .

To a man, Chandler knew, they would see justice was done, to one and all.

The End

– Tom Sheehan

served in 31st Infantry Regiment, Korea, 1951-52, graduated
Boston College, 1956. Poetry books include *This Rare Earth &
Other Flights; Ah, Devon Unbowed* and *The Saugus Book.* He
has 20 Pushcart nominations, 340 stories on *Rope and Wire
Magazine,* work in *Rosebud Magazine* (5), The *Linnet's Wings*
(6), *Ocean Magazine* (8), and many internet sites/print issues/
anthologies including *Nervous Breakdown, Eskimo Pie, Faith-
Hope-Fiction, Subtle Tea, Danse Macabre, Deep South Maga-
zine,* Best of Sand Hill Review, Frontier Tales, Wilderness
House Literary Review, MGVersion2Datura, Dew on the Kudzu,
Literary Orphans, Eastlit, and Nazar Look, etc. His work has
been published in Romania, France, Ireland, England, Scotland,
Italy, Thailand, China, Mexico, Canada, etc.

His latest eBook is *Murder at the Forum,* released January
2013 by Danse Macabre-Lazarus-Anvil Fiction. Two mysteries
are scheduled for 2013: *Death of a Lottery Foe* and *Death by
Punishment.* Other eBooks include the collections *Epic Cures*
(with an Indie Award); *Brief Cases, Short Spans; A Collection
of Friends* and *From the Quickening.* His newest eBooks from
Milspeak Publishers are *Korean Echoes,* nominated for a Distin-

guished Military Award, and The *Westering,*
2012, nominated for a National Book Award
by the publisher.

Now in his 86th year, Sheehan writes 1000
words a day. *Boston Globe's* Alan Lupo
(RIP) said, "Sheehan is Dos Passos
reincarnated and drives a story into our
souls as if it were an old Buick Roadmaster."

THE STOCK DETECTIVE

By Kenneth Newton

The stock detective spotted the cow thieves through his spy-glass from about a half a mile away. He worked his way toward them through a deep gully off to the side, then circled around behind a low hill so he could approach them from the opposite direction without being seen. Near the base of the hill he hobbled his mare, gave her some oats to keep her mind occupied, and pulled a lever action carbine from its scabbard.

He worked his way up the hill with the sun at his back. It was only an hour after sunup; the cow thieves probably thought nobody would get up early enough to catch them, but they were wrong. He crested the hill and watched them for a minute — an old woman and a young man busily quartering a steer. She wielded a long butcher knife, and he worked a cross-cut saw as they hurried to get the carcass into small enough pieces to put into their waiting buckboard.

The stock detective side-stepped and slid his way down the side of the hill, no longer concerned with the element of surprise. He had already achieved that, and he had a Winchester and a top break Smith and Wesson for insurance. Considering that the cow thieves would be looking up into the rising sun, he felt like he had things pretty much under control. "Drop those tools and put up your hands," he said. "I'm arresting you for cattle rustling."

Both of them jerked their heads in his direction and put up a hand to shield their eyes from the sun. If they could see anything, it was just the black silhouette of a man against a hot orange glow, but they knew what was happening. The woman held onto her knife, but the man dropped his saw and glanced quickly toward the seat of the buckboard where a well-worn belt and holster offered up the walnut handle of a Colt percussion revolver some ten feet distant.

"That will be the last stupid thing you ever do," the stock detective warned. There was already a round in the chamber of the carbine. He thumbed back the hammer.

The young man looked back toward the sun. "Now, look, Bull," he said. "This ain't what you think. This is our steer."

"You picked a funny place to butcher him." Bull glanced toward the old woman, who still had her knife but hadn't moved a step. "I said put that down."

The boy was talking again, and reclaimed Bull's attention. "It's the truth, Bull. We had our milk cow bred, and we been raisin' this fella up for slaughter. He broke out. He was pen raised, and didn't know nothin' about makin' his way on rocky ground. When we found him, his leg was broke. You can see it's so."

The steer's right foreleg was broken. Bull gestured toward the back of the buckboard. "For all I know, you did that with that sledge hammer before you brained him with it. Do you reckon I'd find a 36 caliber bullet hole in him someplace, if I was to look?"

"There ain't no bullet in this steer, Bull, and even if there was, without this meat, my grandma ain't gonna make it through the winter."

"Well, let's let the law sort it out."

The young man put his hands to his head in exasperation. "The law? Don't you mean the Cattleman's Association? They own all the lawyers and judges for 100 miles in every direction." He glanced back toward the buckboard.

Bull Henry shook his head. "You're worrying me, boy, the way you keep thinking about going for that gun. You need to give up on that."

The young man's shoulders slumped in resignation, and he turned back toward the stock detective with his arms outspread. "OK, Bull, let's go to town."

Bull pulled the trigger. The boy made it to the buckboard, stumbling backward as he fell, but he was dead before he got there. The woman dropped her knife at last, and ran to the boy's side, sobbing as she fell across his body. Bull walked around her and pulled the old pistol from its holster. After an initial misfire, he shot one round into the carcass of the steer, and another into the hill, then holstered the gun and tossed it into the back of the wagon.

Town Marshal Tom Woodward lifted the blanket and looked at the dead body in the back of the wagon. "Jesus, Bull! Willie Edwards?"

"He fired on me, Tom. It was him or me. Check that cap and ball pistol if you don't believe it."

"I find it damn strange how every man you ever thought stole a steer always took a shot at you and missed, right before you killed him. This was a sweet boy. He wouldn't have shot anybody, not even you."

"Sweet boys don't steal beef cattle."

Woodward walked to the front of the buckboard where Willie's grandmother sat on the seat. "Bertha," he said, "what happened out there?"

She shook her head. "Bull Henry murdered my grandson, that's what, for butcherin' our own steer. But it don't matter none what I say. Bull Henry's with them, and what they say, goes. But there's a higher authority than the Association." She turned in the seat. "And Bull Henry, that authority knows who you are and what you do, and one day, retribution will come."

Woodward saw his teen-age son staring at the body. "You gonna be OK, Jack?" The boy raised his head and looked at Bull

Henry for a moment, then nodded. "All right, then," said the marshal. "You go with Bertha and take Willie to the undertaker, and then you go out there with her and you get what the wolves haven't got of that steer and help her get it home."

"That's a bad idea, Tom," Bull Henry said. "You let one cow thief get away with it and you'll be up to your elbows in cow thieves."

The marshal glanced at the dead man in the wagon. "It's kinda hard for me to see how he got away with anything."

"If she eats Association beef this winter, he got away with it."

Woodward shook his head in disgust. "You stick around town, Bull. This one ain't in the books just yet."

It was in the books as far as Bull Henry was concerned. He went from the marshal's office to the headquarters of the Cattleman's Association, where he collected his bounty. It wasn't strictly legal, but in addition to his generous salary of $100.00 a month, he got $100.00 for every rustler he permanently removed from the range. The association secretary offered to buy him a steak, and an hour or so later, after they'd finished their meal and polished off half a bottle of good Kentucky bourbon, the secretary excused himself. Bull decided to make a night of it and finish the bottle. After all, it was paid for. It had been a good day.

He spent the evening alone at his table, as usual. Some people seemed to have a problem with a man doing his job, and maintaining law and order. Even the cowboys, whose bosses were his bosses, wanted little to do with him. He had his own bunk in every bunkhouse on every spread affiliated with the Association, but he didn't feel wanted in any of them, and was never invited into a game of cards or dominoes. Well, to hell with them. They could have their dollar a day and found. Even Jensen's two dollar women didn't come around offering their company. Bull Henry could buy and sell them by the dozen, but he could do without them, too.

As the night wore on, he dozed from time to time, and sometimes when he came to he had to close his eyes for a moment to stop seeing double, and to try to make the room stop spinning. At one point he felt a hand on his shoulder. "Bull, come on. It's just you and me. If you go home, I can go home." The bartender stood waiting, but when Bull opened his eyes, he didn't see a bartender, he saw Sam Perkins. Half of Sam's head was missing. A 44 caliber slug from Bull's Smith and Wesson had done that job and netted Bull $100.00, but somehow, there stood Sam, big as life, talking about going home. "Whaddya say, Bull, let's call it a night."

Bull stood and threw aside his chair as he backed away from the table and drew his revolver. The man with half a head seemed perplexed. "Whoa, now, Bull," he said, "You don't need that."

"I think maybe I do," Bull slurred, and he shot Sam Perkins through the breast bone. Even if he could live with half a head, he probably couldn't live with a heart shot through and through. It seemed to work, as Sam fell and didn't get up.

The saloon keeper, Nils Jensen, ran out at the sound of the shot. "Holy God, Bull," he said, "you've shot Joe!" But the man confronting Bull Henry was Pete Drake, another rustler he'd seen off. He was bleeding heavily from the chest, but didn't seem much the worse for it. Bull put a bullet between the rustler's eyes and watched him fall.

He then found his way to where the horses were tied. His was the only one there, and as he pulled himself into the saddle, Harvey Flanagan, owner of the Bar D and an Association stalwart, rode up next to him. "What's all the shootin' about, Bull? Did Nils try to get you to pay for your supper?" When Bull ignored the joke and didn't answer, he said, "Well, never mind, come on, and sleep it off at my place."

Bull looked at the man on the horse next to his, and saw the disheveled countenance of Willie Edwards, bleeding from a wound just below his Adam's apple. "You're supposed to be dead."

Flanagan laughed. "You know, Bull, that's what my sweet

young wife says. But she's gonna have to wait a little while longer for the money."

Bull pulled his revolver and began firing wildly at Willie Edwards as he spurred his horse and galloped out of town.

The deputy U.S. marshal looked straight ahead as he rode past the saloon at a slow walk, not offering so much as a sideways glance. Three doors down, he dismounted and tied his horse in front of a dry goods store. He pulled some folded papers from his saddlebag, put them in his coat pocket, and made his way back along the boardwalk. He pushed open the batwings and crossed the room to the bar. As far as he could see, he and the bartender were the only people in the place. That was good.

He put his foot on the rail and leaned on the bar. "Is the beer cold?"

The bartender smiled. "Well, it's slightly cooler than fresh horse piss." He brought up a mug from underneath the bar. "Actually, there's still some ice in the cellar. It's not too bad." He drew a glass and slid it in front of the stranger. "I'm not sure I've had the pleasure." He held out his hand as he eyed the deputy quizzically.

The deputy drained half of the mug before coming up for air. "You're right. That's not half bad." He put down the mug and took the bartender's hand. The man behind the bar was going gray, and he had grown a beard and put on some weight, but the deputy had seen all he needed to see. Releasing the hand, he said, "Keep your hands on the bar where I can see them." He brought up his Colt and removed the wanted poster and arrest warrant from his pocket. He shook the folds out of the papers and laid them on the bar. "Albert Henry — may I still call you Bull? — I'm a federal marshal. I have a warrant for your arrest, not to mention a wanted flyer that says you're worth $100.00, dead or alive."

The bartender kept both hands on top of the bar as ordered. "You're making a mistake, marshal. My name's Bill Clayton, ask anybody around here. The town sheriff will vouch for me."

"There's no mistake. If God Almighty walked into this dump and told me to turn you loose, I wouldn't do it, and there's no higher authority than that. Now come around from behind that bar."

As Bull Henry walked, he gradually turned until his back was to the deputy, and his hands crept slowly toward the edge of the bar. The deputy saw it, and cocked the hammer on the Colt. Bull heard the three ominous clicks and stopped walking. Both hands were now at his sides. "I'm sorry for the things I did, but I just can't go back there," he said.

"You're going to, though, one way or the other."

The deputy thought to himself that Bull was still pretty fast for an old guy — but nobody was fast enough to pick up a sawed-off scattergun, pull back a hammer, turn, and shoot before a man could pull the trigger on a revolver that was already cocked and aimed. He waited until Bull was turned almost all the way around before he shot him. The bullet struck Bull low in the left side and he jerked one trigger on the shotgun as he stumbled around the end of the bar, the load of buckshot splintering a table and chair in the middle of the room.

Bull Henry looked at the deputy as he cocked the other barrel. He had figured out who he was talking to. "Little Jack Woodward. The moustache and scar is what throwed me." He gritted his teeth against the pain.

"Retribution is who I am."

Bull nodded. "Did the wolves get all the beef, or was there some left for the old woman?" He pressed his hand to the wound in the side of his gut.

"Yes, plenty. But she died that winter anyway. Broken heart, they said." The deputy glanced at Bull's bloody side. "That'll kill you, but it's going to take some time, and hurt a lot." He cocked his revolver. "Why don't I — "

Bull raised his bloody hand. "Wait. So, was the steer theirs, after all?"

"It matters now?"

Bull leaned against the bar and nodded. "It does."

"It was theirs. You murdered Willie for nothing, same as the other three."

Bull looked at the floor. "I truly regret it, all of it. If I could make it right, I would."

"That's my job."

Bull raised his head. "Well, then."

"Yeah." The deputy aimed at the middle of Bull's chest and pulled the trigger. One final reflexive jerk on the trigger of the scattergun sent a load of buckshot into the floor as Bull Henry collapsed. The deputy walked over and put another bullet in Bull's chest and one in his head. He heard running footfalls on the boardwalk as he laid the Colt on the bar and retrieved the warrant and wanted poster. Holding the papers aloft in his right hand, and opening his coat with his left to expose his badge, he turned toward the door.

The deputy wrapped Bull Henry's carcass in a tarpaulin and tied it securely in place with a rope, then hopped down out of the back of the buckboard.

The town sheriff sadly shook his head. "That's one of the finest men I ever knew, wrapped up in that tarp."

"I showed you the warrant and the wanted flyer. You saying I got the wrong man?"

"I'm sayin' a man can change."

"Yes, he sure can, but he can't un-do what he's already done. That fine man there killed nine so-called rustlers under color of authority — working as a stock detective for the Cattleman's Association up north — and got away with it. Stock detective was a fancy way of saying hired gun, and a rustler was anybody that owned cattle that didn't pay dues to the Association." Deputy Woodward saw the liveryman coming, and produced a notebook and pencil from his pocket. He began writing as he continued his conversation with the sheriff. "Then he got a little carried away and murdered four men in one day. Even the Association couldn't protect him then, and didn't want to, because one of the four was a big shot Association man named Flanagan. He named Bull as his killer before he died, but Bull was long gone."

"Yeah, everybody, even me, has heard all the Bull Henry stories, includin' how he just disappeared into thin air. My problem is, I can't get used to knowin' that Bill Clayton and Bull Henry was the same man. Bill would give you his last nickel."

The deputy looked up from his notebook. "Bull would give you his last bullet for $100.00."

The stable master had arrived, and he was livid. "Damn you, I told you that rig wasn't for rent."

"And I told you," said the deputy as he continued to write, "I'm requisitioning this wagon and team for official government business. When you retrieve your property in Sheridan and file your claim, you'll be paid a fair rate, plus any legitimate expenses. Your wagon will be stored and your horses boarded for 30 days, after which time they are subject to be sold to the highest bidder as excess government property." He tore the page from the book and held it out to the liveryman. "Don't lose this. It's your only receipt."

He was even madder now. "Sheridan's a hard two days from here. Excess government property, my ass." The stable owner turned to the sheriff. "Carl, don't let him do this."

"I can't stop him, Morgan," replied the sheriff. "Better take your receipt."

Morgan fumed for a few more seconds, then snatched the paper from Woodward's hand and stormed away.

"Why not just leave him here and let us bury him?" asked the sheriff.

"I need proof in order to collect the reward."

"Well, I never understood lawmen collecting bounties. It don't seem right."

The deputy had tied his horse's reins to the buckboard. He now removed the saddle and put it in the bed next to Bull Henry, moving a stirrup to avoid a smear of blood. "Well, your old pal, Bill, would understand," he said with a small grin. "But I suppose I could cut off his head and let you bury the rest, if you want to do that."

"Well, that's a god awful thing to say, but it wouldn't be much worse than what you already did. You damn near shot him to pieces."

"The first bullet went in his gut. The next three were a favor from me to him, to end it quick. But he was a dead man when he grabbed that scattergun. I winged a fella once, when I was young and dumb. I was helping him to the doc's office when he pulled a knife and gave me this for my trouble." His finger traced a long, straight scar on the right side of his face. "Went clear through my cheek, cut my gums to the bone, and took a hunk out of the side of my tongue. Ever since then, if a man turns a weapon on me, I shoot him until he stops moving. Bull wanted to talk a little first, and I had the drop on him, so I let him talk."

"If you'da done me the courtesy of a visit when you got to town, between the two of us we might have arrested him."

"That's one of the things we talked about. He wasn't going back alive."

The sheriff sighed. "How'd you place him here?"

The deputy climbed into the seat of the buckboard. "My daddy and lots of other law dogs, including me, looked for him for ten years off and on, and pretty much gave up on ever finding him. Then just recently, a fella passing through said he knew some-body that knew somebody from down around here that said they thought they'd seen him behind that bar. Damned if they hadn't."

He picked up the reins. "How long has he been here?"

"Two years, give or take."

"I wonder where he was for the first eight." The deputy released the brake. "Wherever he was, he should have stayed there. It's funny to think of Bull Henry getting homesick, and working his way back in our direction." He smiled again.

"Maybe it was Bill Clayton that got homesick."

The deputy raised his eyebrows for a second, then extended his hand. "Yeah, maybe. So long, sheriff."

The sheriff shook his head. "I wish you well, Deputy U.S. Marshal Woodward, but I can't shake that hand."

The deputy withdrew his hand. "Just doing my job, sheriff. If we let one get away with it, God knows how many more will think they can do murder and just ride away."

The sheriff looked at the bloody shape wrapped in the tarp. "Well, he sure didn't get away with it. I reckon nobody ever does. Leastways, not forever."

The deputy clicked his tongue and shook the reins. "I reckon not."

The End

– Kenneth Newton

is a student of the Civil War and the post-war westward expansion, and these interests are reflected in his fiction. He also collects and shoots firearms of that era. He is a member of the Single Action Shooting Society, and participates in the sport of Cowboy Action Shooting. He is a member of Western Writers of America. He has published numerous short stories, in a variety of western venues, and in literary magazines including *Writers*

West, The New Southern Literary Messenger, Unknowns, and *Bane K. Wilker's Tales of the Old West*. His post-Civil War novel, *Passing Through Kansas*, is available on Amazon.com.

He lives in Ridgecrest, California, with his wife Debra and their desert tortoises, Monét and Remington.

WOMEN OF ACTION

By Willy Whiskers; Constable of Calliope, Nevada.

Savanna Sal ran the Peachtree saloon in Calliope Nevada. She had a lively clientele with many would-be suitors among the cowboys and miners who washed the dust from their throats standing at her bar rail. Well-formed and taller than most women, Sal liked pleated dresses that hid a great deal. She had a scar that ran from her right ear across her cheek that she covered with an abundance of makeup.

Each man got a sweet smile and a peck on the cheek, though her heart belonged to Long Jim: gambler, sometimes gun-for-hire and notorious womanizer who held court at a corner table of the Peachtree.

Jim was the handsome sort with a set jaw, thin handlebar mustache that he waxed several times a day and a high-crowned Stetson that accentuated his lean, lanky frame. Favoring a shoulder holster as he felt it preserved a cleaner look when striking a pose at the bar, he carried a white bone-handled nickel plated .38 which he often polished with the ornate silk handkerchief that usually resided foppishly in the upper pocket of Jim's frock coat.

Catercorner across the street from the Peachtree was the professional house of Betsy Lovey. Betsy, who actually did come from Savanna Georgia — as opposed to Sal who did not — was the most prominent madam in the town and Sal's long time rival for Jim's affections.

Madame Betsy was an average woman in height, figure and beauty, but she had a head for figures and could strike a bargain better than any horse trader. This made her one of the richest women in the territory, with interests in mines, ranches and railroads. Still, she was not one to show off, and contented her days tending to her girls and pleasing her customers.

One fine spring morning Betsy woke early and from her bedroom window saw Long Jim standing on the second floor walkway outside Sal's private room, enjoying a cigar. Betsy had dabbled in Jim before and knew all of his angles, but seeing him there — as the sun peeked over the hills illuminating his face — created a desire deep inside. In that instant, she decided to take Jim away from Sal, once and for all.

Quickly changing into a sheer gown, she stepped out onto her own balcony. As she struck a pose of her own that accentuated her best features, she coyly waved at Jim, beckoning him over. With a devious devilish grin, Jim glanced into Sal's room to make sure she was still asleep. He then lightly descended the stairs at the side of the saloon and swaggered across the empty street to Betsy's place.

Few happenings in Calliope escaped Sal's attention. As crafty as Betsy was in business, Sal matched her in intrigue. Aside from booze and good times, Sal's forte was information; who met who behind the cow shed, where to find this body or that, and all territorial goings-on arrived at her door. Her pet name for the Governor was "Sweet Little Joe". So, thanks to her network of spies, Jim's early morning assignation was not as secret as he would have liked. She decided that Betsy's affront could not stand. The situation did not improve when Jim came in that afternoon.

"Where were you this morning? Was surprised you not being there when I got up," Sal asked.

Jim smiled broadly with a little chuckle, "Oh, I had some business, but I'm here now. Where's my kiss?"

The matter festered for a few more days with each woman

conniving ways to dispose of the other. Playing the friendly snake, Sal thought about inviting Betsy over for afternoon tea then poisoning her cup. Betsy scanned her visitors for a likely assassin to surprise Sal one dark night. No matter how deranged the plans, neither of them were satisfied as they were both women of action.

So it came to pass that late one morning Jim accompanied Betsy as she shopped at the town's several mercantiles. Sal saw them through the shop window and decided this was her opportunity. Betsy stepped out onto the sidewalk with Jim following behind, his arms full of packages.

"Jim's mine, clear off!" Sal snapped.

"Clear off yourself, you old harpy. He's mine and he's goin' to stick" answered the working girl, her finger an inch from Sal's nose.

Sal pulled a pocket pistol from her crinolines and sent an errant shot at Betsy's head. Her rival pulled two derringers from her own hiding places and fired them both.

Amazed at her good fortune at not being hit, Sal needed a better location and bolted for the safety of her saloon. Betsy pursued, firing as she ran. Busting through the saloon doors, Betsy saw Sal behind the bar and dodged her fire by diving behind a table. Bang, bang, bang, bang, they traded fire though neither one drew blood. Amid the pistol reports and gun smoke came a silly, sadistic laugh. Behind the swinging doors stood Long Jim applying a fresh pinch of mustache wax and sporting such a smile his face was likely to split. Two women making such a fuss over him amused him greatly.

Sal and Betsy looked at each other crouching in their embarrassing and most unladylike manner. Suddenly clarity overcame them. They could be real and true friends if one difficult impediment they shared could be removed. Pointing their guns at the swinging doors, they blew their troubles away.

– Willy Whiskers

Calliope Gazette, June 18, 1910: For as long as anyone here remembers a bearded gentleman has prowled the streets of Calliope befriending souls, tending to the community's business and extolling the exploits of our residents. Of course we refer to Willy Whiskers; William Holston Bonifantie. We suspect none our readers know Willy by that name. He came to Calliope in 1870 as the engineer of Engine 75 from the old Nevada Central Railroad (NCRR), later he became our beloved constable.

"Couldn't have done my job without him," said retired sheriff Billy Blowbag. "Willy drank a lot of my coffee, but we passed many cold nights listening to him."

"Willy, we love him here," said Savanna Sal at the Peach Tree when we interviewed her and her friend, Betsy Loving. "When Willy gets to telling his tales there's always a lively crown around his table. Most folks are scared of being included in his stories, but they get mighty bent if they aren't."

Our school mistress Mrs. Dorothy McCallian has heard Willy many times. "Willy is like a Homer for all the people. There is no better sight then the light in my student's eyes when he comes to class and talks to them of the old days in Calliope."

When we asked Willy were his stories originate, the normally loquacious yarn-spinner said "Oh, I just tell them like they wish it was." Still making his rounds, we look forward to hearing from Willy for years to come.

REDEMPTION BOUND

by Kenneth Mark Hoover

We rode all day with scheduled stops so the horses could blow. The iron-hot wind sheared off the hard pan and blasted our faces. We had gloves, bandanas and hats pulled down, but the skin around our eyes and wrists were cut from whipping sand and flake rock.

"Damn all motherless lawmen," Cal growled from his saddle. "Hang a man even in this weather."

"Shut up."

I was leading his horse, the extended reins dallied around my pommel, through rough country. I didn't want to tie him fast in this weather. If I fell off a cutbank or into an arroyo I didn't care if Buford came with me. But if he went down first I wanted to be able to slip the knot fast so I wouldn't be pulled in after him.

You think about things like that when lawing on the frontera. Any lawman who doesn't tends to live a short life.

Even all, Buford wasn't as wind-chewed and rock-bit as I was. He sat one of our tough little chestnut mustangs we used to ride prisoners to gallows. His brown hands, horned yellow with calluses and missing two fingers on his left hand from an old hatchet fight, were lashed tight to the cantle. A separate rope dangled from his unshaven neck to the saddle horn. He rode with his big head bowed, letting the wind-driven sand beat against his down-turned Stetson.

"I never know'd a man so fired anxious to watch another

hang," he continued. "You come by this dedication when they
gave you that fancy Marshal's badge?"

"I don't like the dust and wind any more than you, Buford."

"Fooled me."

He didn't speak again for the remainder of the day. Maybe he
didn't have the breath. I know I didn't. That dry, hot wind sucked
the life out until you were nothing but empty husk with eyes.

Not that I blamed him for grousing. Like as not he could already feel the hemp noose cinching around his neck, and wondered how it was to die with blood boiling behind his strangling
face, his body kicking like a fish on a jerk-line.

Not that I felt in any way sorry for Cal Buford, either. He had
shot a man in the back of the head right in front of the Governor's Palace in Santa Fe. He had been arrested, sentenced, and
would be killed in turn. Ordinarily, we didn't do a hanging in
Haxan. But Judge Creighton, in one of his more sober moods,
figured we spent enough money running Buford to ground
through Colorado, Kansas, and finally down to the bed of a con-
sumptive whore in an El Paso cantina.

"We might as well save the taxpayers any further expense,"
Judge Creighton had said over cigars and Kentucky bourbon,
"and stretch him in Haxan."

It wasn't my place to argue. I know some people don't like
hearing this, but I never feel much sorrow for them I ride to
gallows. Which is why the War Department ordered me to the
New Mexican Territory in the first place. Judge Creighton wanted someone as hard as the spoilers who killed and raped their
way across the New Mexican desert. Simply put, he wanted
another murdering bastard who would meet these killers on their
own terms, and take them down.

That's how I got the badge, if it matters.

The hazy sun dipped near the horizon, a great orange ball of
dying flame. With all the sand and dust in the air, nighttime fell
fast. I hobbled the horses in a draw and found shelter in a lime-

stone cave whose opening was ringed with cat's claw and tall ocotillo. It was nestled in the lee of a slanting hogback which gave us further protection from the weather.

There wasn't enough room to stand but we could sit comfortably. There were signs other men had used this shelter before us. The ceiling was blackened with soot and there were scattered animal bones on the floor along with rotten rags and a stone fire ring. I struck a small fire and Cal huddled over it, his long arms draped across his knees like broken willow branches.

We had little to eat except leathery charqui and a tin of biscuits old enough to have been saved from the Mexican war. Despite their good intentions, Washington wasn't long on making sure its federal lawmen were well-paid or living in anything resembling comfort. Ordinary citizens were no better. Like most people they wanted law and order right enough, but they didn't want to actually pay for it in anything resembling money.

I guess it was better than being a Texas Ranger, however. At least I didn't have to buy my own horse.

Still, it felt good to chew something other than sand. After I washed down the crude meal with a mouthful of stale water I started feeling most human again. I packed the bowl of my briar pipe with Virginia Kinnikinnick and fired the tobacco with a burning branch from the fire.

Cal worked the knots and kinks out of his back, grunting with relief. The Pittsburgh iron around his wrists and ankles clinked whenever he moved. I wasn't worried about him escaping. Trussed like that he wasn't going anywhere. And if he tried, he knew I'd put a ball in his back.

"I needed that stretch," he admitted. "That's a hard saddle you gave me." He watched me across the fire with eyes the color of dark syrup. Dust hissed off the top of the hogback and fell in a fine rain beyond the opening. Long blades of light from the dying sun lay outside our cave, mixing with the purple shadows from the cactus and a lone mesquite tree.

Buford tore at the charqui with white teeth on the right side of his jaw. All the teeth on the left side were missing.

"Guess I'll get all the stretching I want when we reach Haxan, ain't that right, Marshal?" He chewed and swallowed, waiting for me to say something.

I shrugged. "Guess so."

Now that night was coming full upon us the wind died down. The storm was abated. In a last blaze of glory the shards of light outside the cave shortened and were swallowed by encroaching shadows of India Ink that dripped from the rocks.

The light of our fire flickered on the low ceiling and rough walls. "Best stop thinking about it, Buford. It will happen soon enough, never mind."

"Mebbe." He studied the piece of buffalo jerky in his fist. "I hate to have to hang, Marshal. Eating is one of the few pleasures all men share. Gonna miss that."

They always want to talk the closer they get to the gallows. I let them. A condemned man should have that much of a right, even if he's nothing but a black murderer like Cal Buford.

During the day I had picked up a mesquite thorn in the back of my hand. I worked it out with the tip of a skinning knife before the poison could take hold.

"No one told you to shoot that Chinaman, Buford," I said.

"The yellow bastard poisoned my best leopard hound, Marshal. I raised that dog since he was a pup. Ain't you never had a dog you liked?"

"I guess I did once't."

"Then you know how I felt."

"Buford, the man was putting out bait to poison coyotes what killed his laying chickens. He didn't know better than to kill your leopard dog."

I folded the skinning knife and put it back in my pocket. "Anyhow, the judge and jury saw it some different than you."

Buford sucked his teeth. "Hell of a thing when a white man can't shoot a Chinaman nowheres he wants. I guess that's what they call civilization now."

"No, Buford, that's what they call simple plain murder."

He watched the dancing tongues of flame and tore another bite of dried jerk with his teeth.

"All you lawdogs are whelped from the same mother," he said around a final mouthful of meat. "You only see the black and white printed words in law books. You forget there are shades of gray in every man's life."

When he finished the charqui he wiped his fingers on his shirt. I handed him the canteen. "Thanks," he said.

"I'll say this for you, Buford. You are more eloquent and philosophical than other men I bring in." I motioned to the canteen. "Two swallows. Water's got to last us until tomorrow."

"What time you figure we'll be in Haxan, Marshal?"

"Toward noon. I know this country pretty well from here on. We'll hit Larsen Valley round midmorning if the weather holds."

He drank his ration and capped the canteen. "And I got to hang three days after that?"

"That's what the execution order says."

We listened to the crackle of the fire and watched the shadows dance like teasing women across the ceiling.

"How many men you done killed, Marshal?"

"My share, I suppose. Why?"

"It never bother you some?"

My pipe had burned out. I knocked the dottle into the fire. "Not much."

I was surprised to see a sort of respectful light take hold of his eyes. "That's a hard thing to say even on a raw night like this, Marshal. Not many lawmen would admit to something like that."

I put my pipe away in my shirt pocket and leaned back against my saddle. "I've been doing this bad job for a long time," I explained. "Someday I will die of it. The men who kill and murder will one day kill and murder me. You must accept that when you pin on the badge. It's all a game of odds, Buford. You can't buck the tiger forever. Eventually, the house wins. That's all."

Buford kicked one of the spindly mesquite branches toward the fire so it would catch. He laughed a bit, but there was more irony in the tone than humor.

"You telling me you are also condemned, Marshal?"

I watched him hard. "Any lawman out here who thinks different is naught but fooling himself. Thing is, I'm not fatalistic about it. I will fight and claw to live, and when my time comes I will die hard and take a hell of a lot of you with me. But I will die, Buford. Like all men. And it's this badge," I tapped the tin, "that will kill me."

Buford opened his mouth to say something, stopped. He waited a good ten minutes before he spoke again.

"When we was kids," he said, "we lived next to an apple orchard. Every morning I sneaked out of bed and stole an apple for breakfast. That's about when I found my pup dog, too. He was a stray with a broken leg and I nursed him good 'til he could run. Anyway, this one morning we had a thick hoar frost on the ground and fence rails. It looked like silver shavings and the air was still like the earth was holding its breath or something. I walked into the middle of the orchard, my pup sniffing my heels. Marshal, I barely put my hand under this here one red apple and like that," he snapped his fingers, "it fell ripe and perfect into my palm."

He held out his hand between us, calloused palm facing the ceiling. "I never ate no other apple as cold and sweet and perfect as that one. I felt a deep shiver run through me like a douse of water. It woke me up, I guess you could say. That's when I knew this world was a fine thing and it was good to be a living part of it. Hell, I never stole no other apple, or anything else, my whole life. I knew nothing I ever did would be as fine and perfect as that one apple, ready to fall at my touch."

His voice dropped low. "All my days I remembered that morning, and how good I felt. Except the night I put the sights of my gun on the back of that Chinaman's head. That's the one time I forgot what it was to stand in that orchard on a cold and frosty morning with the earth holding its breath." He paused. "That's all I have to say, I guess."

Buford lay on the ground, his head resting against his saddle and his hat tipped over his face. I watched the dark sky through the opening of our cave. A patch of night with stars sprinkled like sugar gleamed through a sudden break in the clouds.

The storm had moved on, leaving everything around us quiet except for the snap of the camp fire and our breathing.

The next morning was clear and bright. We rode with the yellow sun on our backs. Our shadows stretched before us like black rails. As we topped a rise we saw Larsen Valley spread out like a rich quilt of water and grass and hard-scrabble farms, with a deep blue sky covering it all.

In the distance I could make out a dark green patch of some kind of regular wood standing firm on the shallow banks of Broken Bow River. Beyond it were the ramshackle buildings of Haxan set hard against the roots of the San Andreas Mountains. You could almost smell the town's rip-sawed lumber, wood smoke and frying tortillas from cooking fires, and choking street dust.

Buford sat his horse beside mine. The sun was behind him, too. His face lay in shadow, but I noted his watchful eyes below the low brim of his hat.

I removed my watch from my vest pocket and flipped the cover. "Going on toward mid-morning," I said. "We'll noon in Haxan for sure."

Buford turned to me. "You called it right on the button, Marshal." He continued to watch me. He was too close to dying to ask for favors.

I put my watch away. "I'm guessing we can stop and rest once more before we ride into town," I told him. I made a forward gesture. "There's an orchard or something down that way. Be a cool rest in the shade of those trees for a minute or two."

Buford didn't grin. He was too close to the gallows to do anything like that. But he was grateful enough to say, "Thanks, Marshal."

I shrugged. "Maybe someday a man will do as much for me when I'm about to die, Buford. Let's go."

I took the reins of his horse while kicking mine forward. We took the slope together, two condemned men, and rode into the waiting orchard with its cool shadows, and deeper secrets.

The End

– Kenneth Mark Hoover

has sold over fifty short stories and articles. His fiction has appeared in magazines such as *Fantastic Stories, Strange Horizons, Challenging Destiny, Three Crow Press* and the new science fiction anthology *Destination: Future*. His first novel, *Fevreblau*, was published by Five Star Press in 2005. His story "Haxan," set in the same world as "White Hawk," appeared in Beneath Ceaseless Skies #13.

    Mr. Hoover currently lives in Dallas, TX.

INDIAN AGENT

by Gary Ives

Amos Merriweather's assignment as Badger Creek Indian Agent was a reward. As a Cavalry Captain at the Battle of Yellow Tavern he had rescued a dismounted major who some said was no more a thrown rider than a pumpkin and actually was a panicked runaway heading off the battlefield lickety split for the tall cotton. But Amos had intervened. He'd seen plenty of men cut and run, most of them good men, and if the major had had a lapse of courage, well, so what. The war was craziness. Let it go. His written report, eventually reaching General Sherman, even earned the Major accolades and a promotion. Now ten years after the war that major was a United States Congressman with higher political ambitions. The congressman's vague notion that Amos Merriweather's knowledge could damage his future led him to seek out Merriweather with the aim get him as far from his congressional district as possible.

Since the end of the war Merriweather had run the livery stable in St. Joseph that he'd inherited from his father, barely managing to keep it afloat. How he hated dealing with customers, generally city men who'd never owned a horse, who didn't know how to saddle, ride, hitch or in any way properly tend a mount much less a wagon or trap. But, oh, didn't they know how to piss and moan and how to try to whittle down a bill. Horses he knew — business he didn't. The appointment, the congressman assured him, was his to assign. Merriweather considered the congressman's offer manna from heaven and asked no questions.

"A $2,000 salary as Indian Agent and another $1,000 as U.S. Marshal. Plus a budget of $5,000 to take care of your redskins. You're a natural for this. These Injuns, they're pretty much pacified since they got their asses kicked back in '62 in The Dakota War... Hand out a few blankets and barrels of flour and keep 'em off the whiskey trail . . . that's 'bout it. You'd be a fool not to jump at this, Merriweather." He agreed and in two weeks received his appointment. He turned the livery stable to his brother and headed west with his bay mare and a string of four pack horses.

Far beyond handing out blankets, his written commission detailed responsibilities "to maintain law and order, to establish schools that would educate the savage in agriculture, and to take all steps to civilize various heathen nations within his administrative confines."

The Station at Badger Creek had been originally built by the army during the war to establish stronger American presence in Sioux territory after the Indian uprising in Wisconsin. Afterwards it served as a horse buying post. Merriweather arrived in May and relieved the last military Indian Agent to begin administration of his various heathen nations.

The captain he relieved advised him where and when to look for the French Canadian drummer who regularly came through to trade whiskey with the tribes. "Arrest that whiskey sellin' rascal and your job will be a hell of a lot easier. The good Lord knows I've had my bellyful of drunken Injuns. Good luck, Merriweather." Perhaps because Merriweather had been a captain himself, or maybe because they just didn't care to dismantle and load them, the blacksmith forge, anvils, and other heavy tools were left behind.

A month later Merriweather struck a secret deal with Pardieu, the trader, which allowed Pardieu access to the tribes in return for a steady supply of whiskey for himself and the caveat that he not cheat the tribes and that he provide intelligence to Merriweather. He told Pardieu, "I don't give a damn how drunk they get or what they do to each other as long as they don't mess with the settlers or the emigrants. Your trade with 'em, as long as it's square, and my blankets and flour are gonna help keep 'em happy." He'd asked him to arrange a powwow with the principal chiefs. Pardieu, who had fretted about the arrival of a civilian Indian Agent, was relieved. While Merriweather had little knowledge of the Sioux or other tribes, it was clear he wasn't stupid. The Sioux chiefs would want to know everything about Merriweather. This placed Pardieu in an ideal position. And that night he gave thanks to the Virgin Mother for delivering Merriweather to Badger Creek.

The powwow, held the next month, lasted several days and nights. Pardieu and Merriweather feasted at a Hunkpapa summer camp on Elk Creek. Much whiskey, dancing and gift giving preceded a rash of promises from both sides and Merriweather returned to his station with a sixteen-year-old Cheyenne captive and adopted daughter of old Crow Face, a generous Hunkpapa chief.

For Merriweather, things couldn't have begun better. Keya, the girl, was a blessing not only to Merriweather's bed but to the station in general. Fluent in Sioux and Cheyenne, she could communicate roughly in Comanche and French also. English came smoothly to her and she had a knack for teaching Merriweather Sioux. The Station had a capable interpreter and was maintained as neat as a military post but with better cooking. Keya appreciated Merriweather's sense of humor and his whiskey and they became close. Whenever Pardieu came through he spent a couple of days at Merriweather's station. Pardieu's wife was Sioux and Mary Big Heart and Keya became good friends. Pardieu always left a cask of whiskey and another of rum for Merriweather.

Merriweather had called on every settler within a twenty mile
radius of the station. As United States Marshal for the 850
square mile territory, he listened to litanies of old complaints:
thefts and swindles that had occurred twenty years ago; property
disputes which he knew the only settlement to be over a grave;
and numerous rustling complaints. Excepting the property
disputes most of the complaints were against Indians. In the
interest of good service he promised to look into this complaint
or that as soon as he could. But when he left a homestead he
generally left the complaint behind. They all complained of a
Frenchman who came down from Canada to trade whiskey for
furs. Merriweather said he'd certainly look for that rascal. The
one common complaint he'd heard from half a dozen settlers
concerned the half-breed Slape Stone, a violent gun-slinger who
took whatever he wanted be it a ham from a smokehouse or a
young girl's virtue. He'd shot three white men and at least three
Indians. The Sioux's complaints were as loud and numerous as
the settlers' and Merriweather decided that killing Slape Stone
on sight would put out that fire and make everyone happy.

He considered most homesteaders childish. Veterans and
farm hands came west with big dreams of fields, orchards, herds
and flocks but without a whit of sense about the hard work, the
winters, or the Indians. More quit their homesteads than stayed
but those who stayed were tough and generally pig-headed.
Settlers had two common complaints against Indians: thieving
and trespassing. Complaints about trespassing he ignored. Early
on he'd learned explanations about the Sioux concepts of land
and hospitality were met with hostility. Merriweather never
minded that the Station always had a few families camped a
stone's throw from the flagpole. The nearest settler to the station
was Jensen, a hard-headed Swede farmer. Jensen had fought the
Sioux in the Wisconsin war in '62 and had no use for Indians. He
asked Merriweather's help to prevent the Sioux from crossing his

land as his wife was terrified by the sight of any Indian. He yelled
at Merriweather telling him he was a fool not to "run dem damn
teeves and beggars off."

Merriweather replied that this was the Indian Agency and he
reckoned when Indians felt welcome they didn't feel like burnin'
and scalpin' folks.

Swenson called him a damned Indian-lover and cursed him,
threatening to write a letter to the Territorial Governor.

With the chiefs, Merriweather arranged for a yearly powwow
in late August at which he would distribute treaty gifts and where
Pardieu would trade. Merriweather's turning a blind eye at the
whiskey and rifle trade pleased most of the chiefs. Pardieu was
generous toward the chiefs themselves and fair in his trades with
all. He had become good friends with Crow Face and won much
favor with the Hunkpapa by shoeing their ponies at the Station.
If a drunk misbehaved and fought or raped, the deed was considered an Indian matter. Merriweather's reluctance to interfere
with tribal notions of justice was a lynchpin in maintaining the
peace. Both parties understood, however, that crimes against
whites would be settled by white man terms. Stealing had to be
confronted and when he was convinced livestock had been stolen
Merriweather went after and sometimes recovered the loss. He
asked the chiefs to provide him with three young men to serve as
Indian police. These men he armed, deputized, and paid $5 per
month. Indians guilty of rustling were punished at the Indian
Agent's whipping post with twenty-five lashes administered by
one of the Indian police. Rape, arson and murder committed on
whites were understood by all as capital crimes punishable by
hanging. Merriweather was thankful that he had yet to deal with
a capital case.

In late summer of the fourth year, passing emigrants delivered a letter notifying Merriweather of the future arrival of a
missionary family who were to assist in the establishment of an
Indian agricultural school at Merriweather's station. He was

directed to provide assistance toward its construction and
development. By now, he and Keya had two baby girls and a
family with children would be welcome. Within two weeks, the
missionaries arrived aboard a wagon drawn by oxen.

Jarvis had been only ten minutes at the station when Merriweather refused his request for Indian laborers. Jarvis asserted
that he'd been assured of the Indian agent's cooperation and, if
that cooperation was not forthcoming, he would report this
matter to Merriweather's superiors.

"Rev. Jarvis, I myself can help you some, but these people will
not leave off their summer hunt to come build you a cabin, or
church, or whatever. Those oxen of yours ought to do you proud
and your wagons'll give good shelter until you're under a roof."

The cabin was to be built on a knoll half a mile downstream
from the station. Initially, he assisted the missionary with felling
the timber for his cabin but quickly tired of Jarvis' constant complaints, laziness, and an unwillingness to listen to good advice.
Mrs. Jarvis, on the contrary, was appreciative of any assistance.
Keya spent time helping the family settle in, teaching the tasks of
their daily routine, fetching water, washing, cooking, etc. The
women enjoyed each other's company. However, once Rev.
Jarvis realized that Merriweather and she slept together, he forbade his wife to associate with "the heathen fornicator."

By late August the cabin's walls were up and the door hung.
One afternoon a rider came to the station with news of the theft
of a calf from a farm on the Little Owl Creek, 100 miles away, and
Slape Stone the suspect. The Jarvis cabin was still without a roof.
Before leaving to investigate, Merriweather advised Jarvis to work
quickly to get the roof up. He offered Keya's help which Jarvis
refused. Three days later, Merriweather arrived at Little Owl
Creek. He picked up Slape Stone's trail but lost him when the
clever rustler backtracked in a rain storm. Merriweather figured,
now that Slape Stone knew he was being hunted, he'd be harder
to corner. At the French Creek trading post, Merriweather wrote

a bill posting a $100 reward for the outlaw.

When Merriweather returned to the Station a week later, little progress had been made. A spread of canvas still served as a makeshift roof. He explained to Jarvis again the urgent need to get his roof finished. He would need the autumn to hunt and bring in enough meat and fire wood for winter. Jarvis simply replied, "God will provide."

"Dammit man, you are lookin' at a cold and hungry winter. God will not cut your firewood. God will not shoot your meat for you. And since God will not shoot your damned meat then I'm pretty sure God will not smoke the meat He isn't gonna shoot for you. Now, I can help you get your ridge pole up and Keya can help your missus and you shave shakes."

"The help of a drunkard, a fornicator, and a blasphemer? No thank you, Mister Merriweather."

"Suit yourself, you goddamn fool."

Later Amos Merriweather, Keya, and their two babies left the post for a week at the powwow. Merriweather's mare had foaled that spring and the colt was a present for Crow Face. The powwow was even more festive than ever. Pardieu's woman, Mary Big Heart, had also given him a son and there was celebration over the children. Pardieu as usual was generous with the whiskey. Before returning to the Station Merriweather had instructed the chiefs to send riders with travois to the station for the distribution of flour, salt pork, and blankets. Crow Face, normally sanguine, was so taken with his grandchildren that he accompanied Merriweather and Keya back to the Station for a visit. Upon their return, all were surprised to see that Jarvis had moved his family into the Station.

"I told you God would provide. How unchristian it would be, Mr. Merriweather, to not share your spacious quarters this winter? I'm sorry if we've had our differences this past summer, sir."

His moving into the station infuriated Merriweather and

presented a dilemma. Sioux custom forbade denial of hospitality
— absolutely. If Crow Face interpreted their eviction as the
breaking of a taboo, Merriweather would lose honor which had
taken years to build. Merriweather resolved to do nothing until
the old Sioux left. Keya was obliged to prepare meals not only for
themselves but for the Jarvis family as well. Some relief came
each evening after supper when Merriweather, Crow Face, and
Keya sat on the porch talking and drinking from the whiskey cask
late into the night. Crow Face asked why Jarvis didn't join the
drinking and storytelling. Was he sick? He wanted Jarvis to
come and join them. He could see Jarvis was ill-prepared for
winter and the old Indian was taken with the little blonde girls.
Crow Face even asked Merriweather if he thought Jarvis would
trade those little girls for furs or ponies. More from a sense of
humor than anything else, Amos Merriweather passed Crow
Face's inquiry to the Reverend Jarvis the very next day.

"God in Heaven. I cannot under any circumstances imagine
anything worse than my precious girls among devil worshipping
heathens. I curse you Merriweather, you are undoubtedly in
league with the same devils that rule these soulless savages.
Curse you, Merriweather, may God curse you!"

When the tribes' representatives began arriving for winter
rations, the nights grew noisier and stretched into the early
morning hours. Drunken men lay around the station until past
noon when drinking would begin anew. Nothing delays departure like drink.

Refused the loan of a horse, Rev. Jarvis walked the seven
miles to the Swede's place and begged a Christian place to lodge
and for help raising his ridge pole. Jensen and his wife welcomed
the company of another so disgusted with the Indian Agent and
his redskins. While he aided the preacher with his roof, the two
commiserated on the sorry state of the Badger Creek Indian
Agency. As they nailed the shakes to the roof, the two men watched in disgust as Indian parties left with travois laden with beans,

flour, salt pork, and blankets. Crow Face left with his sons to begin their band's trek south to winter camp. The missionaries were ordered to leave the station the next day. Merriweather denied the minister's request for an equal ration of flour and salt pork. "These are treaty rations; they're for the Indian nations."

The first snow fell just as Jarvis and Jensen finished the roof. The Jensens and Jarvises celebrated the move into the cabin with prayers and a haunch of venison the Swede provided. Jensen, however, became highly irritated when the minister refused his offer of trade for the Jarvis' wagon. Did this preacher have no gratitude for Swenson's hospitality, for his labor? The refusal broke the nascent friendship and the angry Swede and his wife left the chilly housewarming.

Now the angry preacher was isolated, facing winter with insufficient food and fuel. Merriweather advised him to head back East before winter set in, for the sake of his wife and children, but the stubborn Jarvis retorted that he would rely on God's goodness, which always saw him through. "God damn you sonofabitch — don't you realize there'll be dire consequences if you don't get your wife and girls out of here?"

The first storm blew in late in September. Jarvis's wife took sick. Merriweather asked the preacher to allow his sick wife to move into the station where Keya could tend her close to the stove but the stubborn man of God would have none of it. She was dead within a week.

Once again Merriweather confronted the angry preacher. The wind was howling so that the men had to shout at one another to be heard. "Jarvis, at least let Keya care for the girls. I care not what happens to your sorry ass, but those girls need tending, man."

"I'm takin' them to the Swedes, they'll be tended by Christians."

"You don't even know if Jensen will take them. He was plenty mad at you last I saw. I don't give a shit what you say, Jarvis. I'm takin' those girls, at least for the winter, now move outta my way, you crazy shit."

"By God, I will kill you if you take my girls."

"Move, I say."

Merriweather strode into the cold cabin where the two little girls lay bundled in the same ragged quilt their poor mama had died in. He spoke softly to them and told them he was taking them into the warm station where Keya would fix them hot mush by the warm stove.

Jarvis watched as the wind slammed shut the door to the station, his babies within, taken by this godless station master and his heathen woman. He raised his arms to heaven beseeching God's help in their deliverance. Then, full of rightous purpose, he strode down to his cabin where he fetched his shotgun. With a burning rage he headed against the wind, the long gun cradled in his arms. The wind blew the brim of his hat up and his coat tails flapped as he stepped up to the porch just as a voice boomed from behind.

"I hear you're lookin' for me, marshal." There on a grey mule sat Slape Stone with a .44 rifle pointed at the preacher's chest.

Jarvis swung around, raising the shotgun, and both weapons discharged in one thunderous explosion.

As Merriweather threw open the door, a thick cloud of white gunsmoke swirled around him. There on the porch lay Jarvis. His coat lay open and blood spurted from the hole in his chest. The pulses diminished as the preacher's eyes glazed. Just beyond Merriweather saw a large gray mule sniffing the writhing frame of Slape Stone, struggling amid a froth of blood dripping from his head, trying to crawl on all fours. His face had caught the blast of the preacher's shotgun. Soon the man collapsed. The wind blew dust around the body. Looking down at what resembled a hat full of crushed tomatoes, Merriweather winced and threw the mule's saddle blanket over the corpse.

In the spring, the girls were allowed to choose living with Merriweather and Keya or the Jensens and opted to stay with the Station Agent. That summer they and Merriweather's daughters lived with Crow Face at the Hunkpapa summer camp and by autumn were as comfortable speaking Siouan as they were with English.

The word spread that Indian Agent and U. S. Marshal Captain Amos Merriweather had gunned down the notorious Slape Stone, and a sigh of relief spread throughout the Badger Creek region. Amos said nothing to dispel the error of the rumor.

The End

– Gary Ives

is a retired Senior Chief Petty Officer who lives in the Ozarks
with his wife, two big dogs, a few chickens and guineas where

 he grows apples and writes.
He is a current Push Cart Prize
nominee for his story "Can You
Come Here For Christmas."
His published works may be
read or listened to at
garyives.wordpress.com.

THE DRIVING FLAME

by Greg Camp

The man sat down on the stool and glanced at the barman. He shoved back the shot glass that he was offered and grabbed the bottle of whiskey. He took a pull from it, holding the liquid in his mouth before swallowing.

"God bless all here," he whispered, "for no one else will."

"What's your name?" the barman asked.

"Dowland."

"You called anything else when you're at home?"

"I don't have a home."

"How about your friends—what do they call you?"

"I only have one, and he knows better than to remind me of what I already know."

"You're a hard man to get on with," the barman said. "How'd your friend do it?"

"It took him a war," Dowland answered, pulling back his duster to reveal the two Colt Navys in his belt. "You want one of your own?"

The bar went silent. Dowland felt the men around him looking for a place to watch without getting shot. The barman just shrugged and went back to his glasses.

One pair of shoes stopped behind Dowland, and he eased around to see whose body was about to lie on the floor.

"My name's Stanley," the man said, "and if you would refrain from shooting me, we could have a pleasant conversation at my table."

"Why would either be of any interest to me?"

"Because that bottle will only go so far, and then a man like you will want coffee. I'm buying."

"A man like me?"

"A veteran of the recent events back east."

"You a Pinkerton?" Dowland demanded, his fingers curled an inch above the butts of his revolvers.

"I'm a correspondent," Stanley answered. "I'm here to write a report for the Indian Peace Commission, but that doesn't mean that I can't notice other points of interest."

After relaxing his hands, Dowland let his arms drop to his sides. He stood.

"Over there," Stanley said, pointing at a table against the back wall.

Dowland picked up the bottle and walked over to take a seat, his head resting on the planks behind him. He watched Stanley collect a pair of glasses and come over to join him. There was not anything obviously wrong with this fellow, and he did have good taste. Still, he needed explaining.

Stanley joined him, sitting down in the chair opposite, his back toward the room.

"You don't have any enemies?" Dowland asked.

"Perhaps I do, but you already took the good seat."

"All right, you wanted to talk. What about?"

"I took one look at you and saw a story," Stanley answered. "I just need to find out which one it is."

"What stories?" Dowland's hands rested on his legs. The whiskey bottle sat untouched on the table.

"I saw your belt buckle when you came in, so I could tell that you fought for the South. I take it that you're not one of the galvanized Yankees that General Dodge brought out here to fight the Indians."

"It's good of you to notice that."

"I keep my eyes open when I can."

"No, it's good for you," Dowland said. "Confusing me with a Yankee is a good way to get dead."

"The war's over," Stanley replied.

"Is it? I haven't read my obituary yet."

"May I?" Stanley asked, pointing at the bottle. Dowland nodded. "It's interesting, then, that you'd find yourself here in North Platte just at this moment." He poured two glasses.

Dowland said nothing, but he stared at Stanley. How much had the man figured out?

"I say it's interesting because a particular Union general happens to be here as well."

"That matters to me?"

"It may. An unrepentant Confederate soldier shows up in town just after General Sherman has come with a peace delegation—I'd say that there may be a connection there."

Dowland laid his hands on his revolvers. "Draw."

"Take it easy. I see several stories in you, but I'm not sure which one I'll write." Stanley slowly picked up his glass and took a sip.

"And you have one that you prefer?" Stanley nodded. "Why do you care?"

"Because the public's tired of the story that you came here to make. North and south, they want to read about a good man standing up to wickedness. It would make them feel that the country's going forward again."

"What's in it for me?"

"Let's put it this way. You told me to draw, so I will." Stanley held his hands out with palms open. "I'll pull out a pack of cards, and we'll play stud. The winner decides."

Dowland hesitated, but the man had him. He put his hands on the table. "Deal."

"You want any money to ride on this?" Stanley asked as he shuffled the cards. He put them down next to Dowland, who cut the deck and pushed them back.

"We're betting stories," Dowland answered.

Stanley dealt two cards apiece, one up and one down. His showed a two of hearts. Dowland had a ten of clubs up. He look-ed at his hole card, a jack of clubs. This was the kind of start that promised great things and usually died in its dreams.

"You have the high card."

"When I was fourteen, I arranged with Agnes Richards to meet behind the grandfather live oak near the church during the ser-vice, but I couldn't get clear of my mother. My father heard me making the plan, though, and come Monday morning, he had me out in the far field clearing stumps at the break of dawn. This went on for every day of that week, and each time, he set me to working with the same words: 'No son of mine fails to keep his word, even if his promise is to the Devil.'"

"And a worthy father he sounds," Stanley said. "Mine, well, the less said about him, the better. I did have an aunt who took me in when I was adrift in the world. She made plain to me that no man gets his daily bread for nothing."

He dealt another card to each of them, a ten of hearts to Dow-land and a five of diamonds for himself. "Pair of tens has the bet."

"My father's intention for me was that I would learn a profes-sion in college that would keep me occupied until it was my time to inherit the plantation. A person might say that the War changed all that, but in fact, my schooling left me unfit for any respectable employment. The men of my regiment did elect me captain, but that was likely on account of them wanting someone else to wear the fancy clothes, figuring that lead was attracted to gold, as it were."

"It is, but that never keeps some men from going after it. My days in uniform were not so distinguished. I spent much of the War serving as a clerk on a frigate."

"On the Shenandoah?"

"No, the Minnesota."

"A Yankee, then," Dowland sneered. "You don't talk like one."

"That's because I got my start in Wales and worked for a while in New Orleans," Stanley replied. "I just ended up on a Union ship, and since I could read and write, I was put to work."

"You know what I hate more than a believing Billy?"

"One who just took what came?" Stanley dealt out two more cards.

Dowland glared at the jack of hearts that he had received and then at the deuce of spades in Stanley's cards. This correspondent was getting his story.

"Pair of tens still has the bet."

"My sister married a man from near Savannah. When Marse Robert surrendered, I considered myself free to fight on as I saw best, so I went south to see about her. I've seen men die by the thousands in but a day or two. That is war. What I saw in Georgia was a promenade of the Devil himself.

"My sister and her husband owned a plantation near Fort McAllister. It took me some time, but I found an old man who knew what happened. He watched Hazen's men burn Annie's home with her and my young niece in it.

"Does that satisfy you as to my reason for coming here?"

"It's a good enough reason, to be sure," Stanley answered. "When I was a boy, I was sent to a workhouse on account of my father having died from his drinking. The master of the house, one James Francis, would have astonished Caligula. One day, I had finally had enough, so I beat the man down and left to find my way in the world."

"Francis lived?"

"That he did. For some men, the best punishment is a memory of pain."

Dowland smiled. "I take your point, but for other men, the present pain of eternal fire is the only answer."

"I suppose that we'll all get there eventually," Stanley said. He handed Dowland an ace of spades and gave himself a five of clubs.

"Two pair showing, so the bet's mine."

"At last, I get to hear the story that you want to write?"

"You've heard about the state of affairs in Cheyenne?"

"Hell on Wheels, that's what you newspaper people call such towns."

"A festering pit of criminality," Stanley said.

"That would seem to be just the sort of place to breed more articles for you," Dowland replied.

"But I've written my share of those articles, and much pleasure would it give my readers, if only the foul deeds were confined within the town's borders."

"You do take your time weaving your tales."

"All right, what would you say about a gang of villains attacking peaceful folk, killing the men and practicing all manner of wickedness on the women and children?"

"I would say that someone ought to call them to account," Dowland answered, "and if I were not otherwise engaged, I'd offer myself for the task. But as you seem to have figured out, I have a person of similar character who needs my attention."

"You're forgetting one thing," Stanley said, pointing at the cards on the table.

Dowland turned over his hole card. "Two pair, jacks high."

Stanley picked up his hole card and held it in the air with its back still facing Dowland. "The agreement was that whoever won would choose the story."

"I told you the lesson that my father taught me. No one has ever had cause to question my word since that day."

Dowland watched Stanley flip the card over, revealing a five of hearts. The scribbler had a full house. Dowland's eyes went out of focus, and in his mind flashed the scene of his sister trapped in the burning house. A fire burned inside him as well, but he was bound to do what he had promised.

Dowland rode slowly through the pines along a gentle slope that looked over a creek below. The sun was just rising, and he had seen smoke floating upward from behind a low ridge on the opposite side. Someone was camping there, and anyone for miles around knew about it.

The air was cold, but the trees broke up the light breeze that blew over their tops. He wished that it would change direction, since he wanted to hear the camp before seeing it. His ears strained, but all that came to him was the rustling of the branches. He felt something more, though. Men sneaked through the tall grass along the creekbed, nearing the tents or wagons or bedrolls of the unsuspecting sleepers who would just be waking up. He had raided many a Yankee encampment just that way.

The first shot split the silence, followed by another and another. Leaning forward, he spurred his horse to a trot. The grass near the creek would have let him go faster, but he needed the cover of the trees.

He passed the point where the ridge sank into the water and saw the tepees gathered on the flat patch of grass at the end of the hollow. A boy, some twelve or thirteen years old, ran between two of the tents, carrying a rifle, and Dowland felt the shot before he heard it and saw the plume of red spray into the air as the child dropped to the ground. On the ridge, a man, covered by a brown coat, lay among the rocks, aiming his own rifle at the camp.

Dowland looped the reins of his horse around the branch of a tree and lifted his Sharps carbine off the saddlehorn. In one continuous motion, he pushed the lever forward with his right hand, pulled a linen cartridge out of his saddlebag with his left hand and put it into the chamber, then snapped the action shut at the moment that he had the man in the sights. The range looked to be sixty yards.

He pulled the set trigger, and while doing so, his eyes saw the man turn from Union captain to General Sherman to the man himself. With the coming of that last image, Dowland moved his finger to the firing trigger and squeezed.

The bullet hit with a thud, and the man cried out and fell silent. Dowland did not watch. In a battle, the shot is on target or it is not; the shooter needs to move before that question is answered. He opened the action and blew through the barrel, then pulled the reins off the branch and walked his horse up the slope and to the left.

The fight continued along the creek, and no one seemed to have noticed Dowland. At every gap in the trees, he searched for another target. A man crouched behind a rock on the bank, firing a revolver toward the camp.

Just as before, Dowland loaded and set the Sharps. His mind kept dragging up memories—this time of the first man that he had killed, a Yankee sergeant at the head of a line of supply wagons— and he waited to fire until he saw the man at the rock.

His shot and another cracked across the water in double beat. He dropped the Sharps onto the pine needles at his feet and spun around, cursing himself for a fool while he brought up his Navy revolvers. This gang had its own sharpshooter, and Dowland had not accounted for that.

A glint of light through the branches, some thirty yards beyond him, caught his eye. Dowland saw the muzzle of the other shooter's rifle dip. The man was loading a cartridge, and a bullet would come his way soon.

Dowland dropped the Navy from his left hand, which then swung over to steady his right. He saw the lens of the telescope coming up to aim at him. It glinted again, and he wanted to fire, but the spark of light made him see his sister surrounded by flames. His finger locked in front of the revolver's trigger, then snapped back.

A burst of pain flashed through his head. The light around him shrank into a single tongue of fire and went dark.

The light opened out again around Dowland. He wanted to sit up, but his head ached. The world came into focus, and he saw that he was lying inside one of the tepees. He patted his hands around him, feeling first the blanket under him and then his guns.

So the Indians had won the battle. Of course they had, since he had been moved and was alive. He reached up to touch his head and felt a bandage. His fingers pressed into the cloth, and he winced from the pain.

The flap opened. Dowland turned his head to see a man standing in the entrance, an Indian.

"I am called High Hawk," the man said. He came inside and sat on a blanket on the other side of the fire from Dowland.

"I have you to thank for saving me?"

"Yes, as we must thank you."

"How'd we do?" Dowland lifted himself up to sit on his blanket. He felt dizzy for a moment, but that passed.

"You killed three, and we killed two more," High Hawk answered. "We lost three, a boy and two men."

"I saw the boy get shot by the man up on the ridge. How many are in this gang?"

"Sometimes more, sometimes fewer. They are like the grass. We cut down one, and three come in his place. We do not grow so well."

"It's the railroad. It brings all kinds out here," Dowland said.

"Did it bring you?"

"In a manner of speaking. The railroad brought General Sherman, and I followed him."

"The maker of war comes to talk peace with us—yes, I know of this general," High Hawk said.

"His men killed my sister and her child. That's how I know him."

"I served under Stand Watie. We heard stories about what Sherman did to Georgia."

"But Watie's regiment was mostly Cherokee. What brought you to it?"

"We saw blue coats on the plains long before the war. The Yankees put one hand into your homes, while the other stretched out toward our lands."

Dowland stared at the ground. His head ached too much to boil with rage, but he could feel its heat rising.

"I wondered if you were telling the truth," High Hawk said. "We have been visited by helpful white men many times. But your rifle and your face speak the same way. Can you stand?"

"Ask me when I've done it."

High Hawk stood and held his hand out to help Dowland, who took it and worked his way up. "You need food." He led the way out of the tepee.

The mention of food brought the odor of soup to Dowland's awareness. At the center of the camp, a large cooking sack hung over a fire. Yes, he was hungry. He had eaten a little before the attack, but that had been before dawn, and it was now early afternoon. He followed High Hawk over to the fire and sat on the ground near him.

A girl filled a bone cup with the soup and handed it to Dowland. She was young, ten years old or so, and to his eye, the flames danced around her in anticipation. He shook his head and took a sip from the cup.

"My daughter," High Hawk said.

Dowland smiled at her. "Thank you."

She looked once at him and then stared at the ground. High Hawk said something to her in their language, and she left.

"Her mother was killed in the first attack during the spring, and her brother died today."

"Is there a leader of this gang?"

"He's a great brute of a man named Duncan MacKenna. From the stories we have heard, at some time, he worked on the railroad, but he has discovered an easier path to fill his belly."

The soup steamed in the chill air, and Dowland stared into it before taking a drink. "Do you know where they hole up?"

"I haven't seen their camp with my own eyes, but they fled upstream, and I know of a cave that way near the water with good grass around it."

"A cave? That's not good. There's only the one way in?"

"No, it is like a tepee. It has a narrow opening to the sky at the rear."

Dowland contemplated the fire, then took another drink of soup. "We hit them tonight. They'll be drunk, licking their wounds. We'll have an end to this."

Dowland and High Hawk crept among the trees and rocks just back of the ridgeline. They were both burdened with short cedars that they had cut earlier. Night had fallen, and the moon was not yet up.

By starlight from behind and a faint glow from beneath, Dowland saw smoke rising from the ground ahead of him. He came within a few feet of the opening and lay down, rolling over to ease the tree off his back and onto the ground. He crawled over to where High Hawk had done the same.

"When the moon rises above that boulder," he whispered, "set light to these, and shove them down. After that, throw in anything you can scrape up. When you hear my third shot, come join me."

"Don't shoot me as I come down the slope."

Dowland grinned and left. He worked his way down through the trees toward a large fir that stood on the edge of the meadow. He climbed into its branches and unslung his Sharps, then prepared the first shot.

He froze in place, the forestock of his rifle resting on his left fist that was lodged on a branch. He glanced occasionally at the ridgeline, watching for firelight.

A man crossed the meadow with a pot and returned with slower step. Dowland saw three others near the mouth of the cave. No one looked like the description of MacKenna, but perhaps he was deeper inside.

Light danced twice at the mouth, and smoke puffed out in heavy exhalations. The gang ran out, and Dowland fired, dropping the man who had carried the pot. Four others doddered about, running a pace back inside, then again toward Dowland, who reloaded and fired a second shot.

His bullet hit a scrawny fellow at the rear of the group, the only one who had thought to pick up a rifle in the confusion. The three who remained scurried behind rocks. Dowland opened the action of his Sharps and blew through the barrel, all the while looking for a target. The smoke now poured in a steady cloud out of the cave.

He saw a man's leg sticking out from one of the rocks. He inserted a new cartridge into the breech and closed the action, cocked the hammer, and set the trigger. The vision of streaming smoke and light made him want to get lost in his thoughts, but he fought down his imagination and fired.

The man sprung into the air screaming, then fell back onto the rocks. The lower half of his leg lay still beneath him.

Dowland reloaded, but before he could take another shot, he heard a crack from the slope and saw the wounded man subside. High Hawk fired a second round from his Henry, and now only one of the gang was still alive in the cave's mouth. That last man made a run for it, which Henry and Sharps together put a stop to.

High Hawk eased his way down the slope to the mouth of the cave, and Dowland climbed out of the tree and joined him.

"I don't see the man you described as the leader." He lowered himself to the ground and crawled into the cave. The air was thick, but he could see well enough to know that no one was hiding inside. He leapt up and ran back out. "We missed MacKenna," he shouted between coughs.

The two men looked at each other, then took off running for the Indian camp.

Dowland gripped High Hawk's shoulder, holding the man back. Women and children were running about in the light of the camp's fire, but the men were gone. Dowland wanted a look at the activity before he rushed into the middle of it.

"Slowly," he said, letting go of High Hawk and working his way forward with a Navy revolver drawn.

A woman running between two tepees saw him and stopped short, a look of terror on her face. She then saw High Hawk and shouted something in her language. He answered her, and they talked for a moment.

"She says that MacKenna came here and took my daughter away up the ridge. The men have followed them."

High Hawk led the way up through the boulders toward the top where three men crouched with their rifles. When Dowland came along beside them, one turned to stare at him.

"Cousin, where are they?" High Hawk asked.

"The white man and your daughter passed along the path through those rocks," the man answered. He pointed at Dowland. "He keeps calling for his brother."

Dowland ignored this and looked behind him. The moon was setting, and dawn was soon to come. His head ached. He turned back to look at the gap in the rocks twenty paces ahead of him. "MacKenna, are you there?" he shouted.

"Is that the white man I saw? What's your name, Injun lover?"

"Dowland."

"Well, Mr. Dowland, come here where I can have a look at you."

Dowland stood and stepped forward. "Send out the girl, and you and I will settle this like men."

"And I suppose your friends will all just go back down the trail?"

"It's their land. They may do as they please on it."

"Not for long, you bastard. And for now, all of you will do what I say. The girl goes nowhere until I see you."

A vision of a burning house shimmered before him, but he

walked toward the gap, holding his hands out flat at his sides. He passed the rocks and turned to see MacKenna a little way up, holding the girl under his left arm, a knife at her throat. He had a Remington revolver in his right hand pointed at Dowland.

"So that's what an Injun lover looks like. Let me watch you drop those guns of yours."

Dowland knelt.

"What, don't want to hurt those precious pretties?

He unbuckled his gun belt, and it and his Navys dropped to the ground.

"Now stand. You did say you wanted to do this like men."

As he rose, his right hand darted into his coat and pulled out a Colt police revolver from the side pocket that he had sown into his vest. The light of dawn bathed MacKenna and the girl in its glow, and Dowland fired. He watched the two of them sink onto the earth, and for a moment, the light looked like flames around his niece.

He ran to the girl and picked her up. She was spattered with MacKenna, but she was alive. He carried her back and put her into her father's arms. He then turned to face High Hawk's cousin.

"That man was not my brother," he said, then walked back to collect his guns.

Dowland sat again with his back to the wall of the saloon, staring at the glass of whiskey in front of him. His sister and niece were dead, and nothing that he could do would change that.

He glanced across at the door to see Stanley coming in, who looked back and came over to sit down across from him.

"You've returned. What happened?"

"I finished the story," Dowland answered.

"Would you care to tell it to me?"

"No."

"I see," Stanley said. "We did have an agreement."

"I agreed to play out whatever story the winner of our card game wanted. I did that. You weren't there, and I don't want to repeat it." Dowland took a sip of his whiskey. "I see that Sherman has returned to Washington."

"Yes, he was called back, and the Peace Commission went on without him. I got a few good articles out of that."

"I figured that you could find a story somewhere, with or without me."

"I can, but I have to say that you'd make an interesting traveling companion," Stanley said. "My paper likes my work, and it occurs to me that I could find some stories in Africa that need writing."

"And much good may it do you," Dowland replied. "As for me, I have business here."

"Some things are better left to themselves."

"Yes, and that's the hard part of life, deciding what is what. Good luck to you, Mr. Stanley."

Stanley nodded and left. Dowland picked up the glass, but then set it back down on the table. Looking into the whiskey, but seeing only the blood of every man that he had killed, he wondered if anything could change his desire for revenge.

The End

– Greg Camp

was born in the hills of North Carolina about a hundred thirty years later than was good for him. He has wandered around the southern United States ever since, picking up bits of experience and polishing his curmudgeonly persona.

He listens to the Muses whenever they sing to him. Following a star brought him and his cat to northwest Arkansas, where he is currently trying to repair his sextant.

Greg has written numerous published short stories and his first science fiction novel, *Draft of Moonlight*, was released by Willow Moon Press in 2013.

Since his feline companion refuses to work for a living, he has to teach English literature and composition to college students and sell his writing on street corners. Free samples can be read here:
http://englreadingandwriting.wordpress.com/
or here:
http://gregorycamp.wordpress.com/
or on Twitter @GregCampNC.

FROM THE EDITOR

Aren't stories wonderful? To be able, for a while, to travel back in time, to go to the far corners of the country, or even the world, to live great adventures, meet fantastic people, see historic events unfold right in front of your eyes? All that, and more, comes from the mind of a storyteller. My first storyteller was my grandmother. She introduced me to the wonderful world of words, words used to paint pictures in my mind. More vivid than reality, her tales allowed me to go out and fight villains and ride monsters. Heady stuff!

Grand as that was, in a way I'm even luckier now. The stories I have now are written. Instead of traveling miles to my grandmother's house, then waiting for her to have time to sit down and regale me with her latest twist on *When Grandpa Shot the Whale*, now I can just sit back in my easy chair and pick up a book, eReader, or laptop. So many books, with so many wonderful stories in them.

Readers are all lucky. From now on, whenever you want, you can pick up this book and take a trip back to the old West, where justice had nothing to do with the law, and a person's word was his bond. Or you can visit www.FrontierTales.com for fresh Tales each month.

I am very grateful to all the Western writers who submit their lovingly-crafted stories, and to every reader who visits each month and votes for his or her favorite Tale. Without all of you, FrontierTales.com would not exist.

So keep on writing, reading and voting, tell your friends about us, and maybe buy a paperback or eBook collection of the "Best of" now and then.

Thanks and Happy Trails to you!

Duke

FRONTIER TALES EZINE

The ezine Frontier Tales was born out of frustration. I couldn't find anywhere to send my Western stories and Dusty Richards, who has over 100 published books under his belt, told me there was much uncertainty facing authors because of the changes in the publishing industry. Book stores were going out of business and magazines were almost a thing of the past. The year 2009 was a scary time for writers.

I was just a beginner at this fiction-writing business, but I knew what we needed. I decided to create an online magazine devoted to Western short stories, and **Frontier Tales.com** was born.

Hundreds of stories have now seen the light of day and a lot of writers, new as well as veterans, have gotten exposure they wouldn't have otherwise found. Several of them have told me that Frontier Tales has made the difference in their writing careers. I'll confess, that makes me proud. Since its beginning, stories from men and women who also love words, ideas, and history have been available to anyone who has a few minutes to take a trip back to the Old West.

Frontier Tales has received a wonderful reception and reaches viewers from around the world, with readership almost doubling every year. If you're a writer, greenhorn or old hand, consider sending us your polished western frontier prose.

The Best of Frontier Tales Anthology, Volume 1 featured the stories from the first year that were voted Favorite of the Month. Now, here's the next year's Best. Enjoy!